RETURN TO
GROOSHAM GRANGE
THE UNHOLY GRAIL

ANTHONY HOROWITZ

RETURN TO
GROOSHAM GRANGE
THE UNHOLY GRAIL

PHILOMEL BOOKS

PHILOMEL BOOKS
A division of Penguin Young Readers Group.
Published by The Penguin Group.
Penguin Group (USA) Inc., 375 Hudson Street, New York, NY 10014, U.S.A.
Penguin Group (Canada), 90 Eglinton Avenue East, Suite 700, Toronto,
Ontario M4P 2Y3, Canada (a division of Pearson Penguin Canada Inc.).
Penguin Books Ltd, 80 Strand, London WC2R 0RL, England.
Penguin Ireland, 25 St. Stephen's Green, Dublin 2, Ireland
(a division of Penguin Books Ltd).
Penguin Group (Australia), 250 Camberwell Road, Camberwell, Victoria 3124,
Australia (a division of Pearson Australia Group Pty Ltd).
Penguin Books India Pvt Ltd, 11 Community Centre, Panchsheel Park,
New Delhi–110 017, India.
Penguin Group (NZ), 67 Apollo Drive, Rosedale, North Shore 0632,
New Zealand (a division of Pearson New Zealand Ltd).
Penguin Books (South Africa) (Pty) Ltd, 24 Sturdee Avenue, Rosebank,
Johannesburg 2196, South Africa.
Penguin Books Ltd, Registered Offices: 80 Strand, London WC2R 0RL, England.

First published in Great Britain by Methuen Children's Books, 1988.

Published simultaneously in Canada. Printed in the United States of America.
Design by Katrina Damkoehler.

Library of Congress Cataloging-in-Publication Data is available upon request.
ISBN 978-0-399-25063-7
10   9   8   7   6   5   4   3   2   1

For Cassian

Contents

TOP SECRET

To the Right Reverend Morris Grope

Bishop of Bletchley

Dear Bishop,

I have now been at Groosham Grange for three months. I've had a terrible time. The teachers here are all monsters. The children are evil . . . and worse still, they enjoy being evil. They even get prizes for it! I hate having to pretend that I like it here, but of course it's the only way to be sure that nobody finds out who I really am.

But all the time I'm thinking about my mission, the reason you sent me here. You wanted me to find a way to destroy the school and the island on which it stands. And the good news is that I think it can be done. At last I have found a way.

It seems that all the power of Groosham Grange is concentrated in a silver cup. They call this cup the Unholy Grail. It's kept hidden in a cave—nobody can get close to it. But once a year it's taken out and given as a prize to the boy or girl who has come out tops in the school exams. This will happen just a few weeks from now.

I've also been doing some research. Looking in the school library, I found an old book of sorcery and spells. In the very back there was a poem. This is what it said:

BEWARE THE SHADOW THAT IS FOUND
STRETCHING OUT ACROSS THE GROUND
WHERE SAINT AUGUSTINE ONCE BEGAN
AND FOUR KNIGHTS SLEW A HOLY MAN
FOR IF THE GRAIL IS CARRIED HERE
THEN GROOSHAM GRANGE WILL DISAPPEAR

And now the good news, Your Holiness! I've worked out what the poem means. And if I can get my hands on the Grail, then I will have accomplished my mission and Groosham Grange will be no more.

With best wishes to you and to Mrs. Grope,
Your obedient servant,
Secret Agent at Groosham Grange

It was Sports Day at Groosham Grange—the egg-and-spoon race—and the egg was winning. It was running on long, elegant legs while the spoon struggled to keep up. In another corner of the field, the three-legged race had just been won, for the second year in a row, by a boy with three legs, while the parents' race had been canceled when someone remembered that none of the parents had actually been invited.

There had been one unfortunate incident during the afternoon. Gregor, the school porter, had been disqualified from javelin throwing. He had strolled across the field without looking, and although he hadn't actually entered the competition, one of the javelins had unfortunately entered him. Mrs. Windergast, the school matron, had taken him to the sick bay with six feet of aluminum jutting out of his shoulder, but it was only when he got there that she had discovered that he couldn't actually get through the door.

Otherwise everything had gone smoothly. The teachers' race had been won, for the third year in a row, by Mr. Kilgraw (dressed in protective black clothing) and Mr. Creer. As one was a vampire and the other a ghost, it was hardly surprising that the race always ended in a dead heat. At four o'clock, the high jump was followed by a high tea: traditionally, it was served on the school battlements.

If anyone had happened to see the sixty-five boys and girls gathered together along with their seven teachers around the sandwiches and strawberries and cream, they would have thought this was an ordinary Sports Day at an ordinary school . . . even if the building itself did look a little like Frankenstein's castle. Looking closer, they might have been puzzled by the fact that everyone in the school was wearing, as well as their sports clothes, an identical black ring. But it would only be if they happened to catch sight of Mr. Fitch and Mr. Teagle, the two heads of Groosham Grange, that they might begin to guess the truth.

For the heads of the school were just that. Two heads on one body: the result of an experiment that had gone horribly wrong. Mr. Teagle, bearded and wearing a straw hat, was eating a cucumber with a pinch of salt. Mr. Fitch, bald and hatless, was chewing a triangle of bread with a little butter. And the two men were both enjoying what would be a perfect sandwich by the time it disappeared down the same, single throat.

Of course, Groosham Grange was anything but ordinary. As well as the ghost, the vampire and the head with two heads, the teachers included a werewolf, a witch and a three-thousand-year-old woman. All the children there were the seventh sons of seventh sons and the seventh daughters of seventh daughters. They had been born with magical powers and the school's real purpose was to teach them how to use those powers in the outside world.

"So what's the last race?" Mr. Teagle asked, helping himself to a cocktail sausage. The wrinkled sausage at the end of its long wooden stick somehow reminded him of Gregor after his recent accident.

"The obstacle course," Mr. Fitch replied.

"Ah yes! Good, good. And who are the finalists?"

Mr. Fitch took a sip of plain black tea. "William Rufus. Jill Green. Jeffrey Joseph. Vincent King. And David Eliot."

Mr. Teagle popped two sugar lumps and a spoonful of milk into his mouth. "David Eliot. That should be interesting."

Ten minutes later, David stood on the starting line, surveying the course ahead. The obstacle course would be, he was certain, like no other obstacle course in the world. And he was equally certain that he would win it.

He had been at Groosham Grange for almost a year. In that time he had grown six inches and filled out a bit, so he looked less like a street urchin, more like a sprinter. He wore his brown hair long now, thrown back off a face that had become paler and more serious. His blue-green eyes had become guarded, almost secretive.

But the real changes had been happening inside him. He had hated the school when he had first arrived . . . but that had been before he discovered why he was there. Now he accepted it. He was the seventh son of a seventh son. That was how he had been born and there was nothing he could do about it. It seemed incredible to him that once he had fought against the school and tried to escape from it. Today, a year later, he knew that there was nowhere else he would rather be. He belonged here. And in just two weeks' time he knew he would walk away with the school's top prize: the Unholy Grail.

There was a movement beside him and he turned to see a tall, fair-haired boy with square shoulders and a smiling, handsome face, walking up to the starting line. Vincent King was the newest arrival at Groosham Grange. He had only come to the school three months before, but in that time he had made astonishing progress. From the moment the school's secrets had been revealed to him and he had been awarded his black ring, he had surged forward, and although David was well ahead in the school exams, there were some who said that Vincent could still catch up.

Maybe this was one of the reasons why David didn't like the other boy. The two of them had been in competition from the very start, but recently the sense of competitiveness had bubbled over into something else. David mistrusted Vincent. He wasn't sure why. And he was determined to beat him.

David watched as Vincent stretched himself, preparing for the race. Neither of them spoke to the other. It had been a while since they had been on talking terms. At the same time, Jill Green strolled over to them. Jill was David's best friend—the two of them had arrived at the school on the same day—and he was annoyed to see her smile at Vincent.

"Good luck," she said.

"Thanks." Vincent smiled back.

David opened his mouth to say something, but then Jeffrey and William arrived and he realized it was time to take his place on the starting line. Mr. Kilgraw—who taught Latin—appeared, carrying a starting gun in his black-gloved hand. The rest of the school was standing a short distance away, watching.

"Take your places," the Latin teacher said.

He raised the gun.

"Sistite! Surgite! Currite . . . !"*

He fired. Five hundred feet above him, a crow squawked and plunged to the ground. The race had begun.

The five runners set off along the course, racing down

----

*Ready, set, go!

the green to the first obstacle—a net hanging about ninety feet high from a wooden frame. Jeffrey had taken an early lead, but David was amused to see him make his first mistake and start climbing the net. For his part, he muttered a quick spell and levitated himself over it. William and Jill turned themselves into dragonflies and flew through it. Vincent had dematerialized and reappeared on the other side. The four of them were neck and neck.

The second obstacle in the race was a shallow pit filled with burning coals. All the children had studied Hawaiian fire walking and David didn't even hesitate. He took the pit in eight strides, noticing out of the corner of his eye that William had forgotten to tie one of his shoelaces and had set fire to his Nike sneaker. That left three.

With the cheers of the rest of the school urging them on, David, Jill and Vincent twisted around the oak tree at the end of the course and disappeared completely. How typical of Mr. Creer to sneak a dimensional warp into the race! One second David was running past the tree with the cliffs ahead of him and the grass swaying gently in the breeze, the next he was battling through a cyclonelike storm of wind and poisonous gases on a planet somewhere on the other side of the universe. It had to be Jupiter from the look of it. Sixteen moons hung in the night sky over him and the gravity was so intense that he could barely lift his feet. The smell of ammonium hydrosulfide made his eyes water and he was glad that he had reacted quickly enough to remember to hold his breath.

He could hear Jill catching up with him, her feet scrunching on the orange-and-gray rubble of the planet's surface. Glancing quickly over his shoulder, he also saw Vincent, rapidly gaining ground. He staggered past the remains of a NASA space probe, heading for a flag that had been planted about a three hundred feet away. His teeth were already chattering—the planet was freezing cold—and he cried out as he was hit by a primordial gas cloud that completely blinded him. But then he was aware that there was grass under his feet once again, and opening his eyes, he saw that he was back on Skrull Island. He had passed the third obstacle. The finish line was ahead. But there were still three more challenges before he got there.

He looked back. Jeffrey and William were far behind. Vincent had overtaken Jill and was only about fifty feet away. With his attention on the other boy, David

12

almost ran straight into the giant spiderweb that was the next obstacle. It had been spun between two trees, almost invisible until you were in it, and David had to twist desperately to avoid the threads. Even so, a single strand—thick and sticky—caught his arm and he had to waste precious seconds tearing it free. Somehow, though, he managed to get through. He tumbled to the ground, somersaulted forward, then got up and ran.

"Come on, Vincent! You can do it!"

David knew that there were as many people cheering him as there were Vincent. But it still irritated him to hear Vincent's name being called out by his friends. His anger spurred him on and he easily cleared the six hurdles ahead of him without even thinking about the ten thousand volts of electricity to which they were connected. That just left the bottomless pit with two narrow planks to carry the runners on to the end.

His foot hit the left plank. It was less than three inches wide and bent slightly as it took his weight. David swayed as he fought to regain his balance and that was when he made his second mistake. He looked down. The pit ran all the way through the center of the earth and out the other side. One slip and he would find himself in New Zealand. David had never been fond of heights and right now he was suspended over what looked like an impossible elevator shaft, though without the advantage of an elevator. Again he had to waste time fighting off the rush of dizziness and nausea. And that was when Vincent overtook him.

David didn't even see the other boy. He was aware only of a shape rushing past him on the other plank. Biting his lip, he forced himself forward. Ten steps, the wooden surface bouncing and bending underneath him, and then he had reached the other side with Vincent between him and the finishing line. Meanwhile, Jill had caught up. She had taken the same plank as David and she was so close that he could almost feel her breath on the back of his neck.

With one last effort, David pushed ahead. The red tape that would end the race was fifty yards ahead. Vincent was just in front of him. The cheering spectators were on both sides, Mr. Kilgraw holding a stopwatch, Mr. Fitch and Mr. Teagle applauding and Mrs. Windergast giving mouth-to-mouth to the injured crow.

David didn't know what he was going to do until he did it. He was still holding the strand of spiderweb, and with a flick of his hand, he threw it in front of him. Even if anyone had been close enough to see what he had

14

done, it might have looked like an accident, as if he had just been trying to get rid of it. The piece of web twisted around Vincent's left ankle and hooked itself over his right foot. It wasn't enough to stop him, but it made him stumble, and at that exact moment David overtook him and with a final gasp felt the tape of the finish line break over his chest.

It was over. He had won.

The entire school went crazy. Everyone was yelling now. David collapsed onto the soft grass and rolled onto his back, while the clouds, the people and the fluttering tape spun around him. Vincent thudded to a halt, his hands on his thighs, panting. Jill had come in third, William fourth. Jeffrey had managed to get himself stuck in the web and was still hanging in the air some distance behind.

"Well done, David!" Mr. Creer was standing by the finish line with a ghost of a smile on his lips. But all his smiles were quite naturally ghostly. "Well run!"

David had beaten Vincent, but he felt no pleasure. As he got to his feet, he was ashamed of himself. He had cheated in front of the entire school, he knew it, and it only made him feel worse when Vincent came over to him with an outstretched hand.

"Good race," Vincent said.

"Thanks." David took the hand, wishing he could undo what he had just done but knowing that it was too late.

He turned to find Jill looking at him strangely. Of course, she had been closest to him when it happened. If anyone could have seen what he'd done, it would have been her. But what would she do? Would she tell?

"Jill . . ." he began.

But she had already turned her back on him and now she walked away.

David was sitting on a long, rocky outcrop, with the cliffs rising up behind him and the sea lapping at his feet. It was one of his favorite places on Skrull Island. He loved the sound of the waves, the emptiness of the horizon, with the great bulk of the Norfolk coastline a gray haze somewhere beyond. He would sit here with the wind rushing at his cheeks and the taste of sea spray on his lips. This was where he came to think.

Twenty-four hours had passed since Sports Day and the excitement of the obstacle course, and in all that time his mood hadn't changed. He was depressed, disappointed with himself. There had been no need to win the race. There were no prizes or cups given out on Sports Day. So what reason did he have to cheat?

"Vincent King . . ." he muttered to himself.

"What about him?"

He looked around and saw Jill Green walking toward him. She had changed as much as he had in the year she had been at Groosham Grange. She was quieter, more relaxed . . . and prettier. With her long dark hair and pale skin, she looked rather like a young witch, which was, of course, exactly what she was.

She sat down next to him. "I can't believe what you did yesterday," she said.

"You saw . . ."

"Yes."

"I was stupid." David was glad she had brought up the subject even though he was almost too ashamed to talk about it. "I didn't mean to do it." He sighed. "But I couldn't let him win. I just couldn't. I don't know why."

"You don't like him."

"No."

"But why not? Vincent's bright. He's popular. And he's very good-looking."

"That's why I don't like him," David said. He thought

for a minute. "He's too perfect altogether. If you ask me, there's something funny about him."

"And if you ask me," Jill said, "you're just jealous."

"Jealous?" David picked up a loose stone and threw it into the sea. He waited until it had disappeared, then reached out with one hand. The stone rocketed out of the water and slapped itself back into his palm. He handed it to Jill.

"Very clever," she muttered sourly.

"Why should I be jealous of Vincent?" David said. "If you're talking about the Unholy Grail, he hasn't got a chance."

"He's only thirty points behind you. He could still catch up."

There were just two weeks until October 31—Halloween—the most important day in the school's calendar. For this was when the Unholy Grail would be presented to the new Student Master. Throughout the year, all the marks from all the exams had been added up and published on a standings list that hung on a wall outside the heads' study. David had been top of the list from the start.

But Vincent had risen so fast that his name was now only one below David's, and although everyone agreed the distance between them was too great, nothing was ever certain, particularly in a school like Groosham Grange. There was, after all, one exam still to go— Advanced Cursing. And David had to remember, it was also possible to lose points. You could have them deducted for bad behavior, for being late . . . and for being caught cheating in a Sports Day race.

"Do you like him?" David asked.

"Yes."

"Do you have a crush on him?"

"That's none of your business." Jill sighed. "Why are you so bothered about him?"

"I don't know." David shivered. The waves were whispering to him, he was sure of it. But he couldn't understand what they were saying. His hand felt cold where it had touched the stone. "There's something wrong about him," he said. "Something phony. I can feel it."

In the distance, a bell rang. It was a quarter to four, almost time for the last two classes of the day: French with Monsieur Leloup, then general witchcraft with Mrs. Windergast. David wasn't looking forward to French. He was almost fluent in Latin and spoke passable Ancient Egyptian, but he couldn't understand the point of learning modern languages. "After all," he often said,

"I can summon up fourteen demons and two demigods in Egyptian, but what can I ask for in French? A plate of cheese!" Nonetheless, Groosham Grange insisted on teaching the full range of academic and college-prep subjects as well as its own more specialized ones. And there were serious punishments if you traveled forward in time just to miss the next class.

"We'd better move," he said.

Jill took hold of his arm. "David," she said. "Promise me you won't cheat again. I mean, it's not like you . . ."

David looked straight into her eyes. "I promise."

Ahead of them, Groosham Grange rose into sight. Even after a year on the island, David still found the school building rather grim. Sometimes it looked like a castle, sometimes more like a haunted house. At night, with the moon sinking behind its great towers to the east and west, it could have been an asylum for the criminally insane. The windows were barred, the doors so thick that when they slammed you could hear them a mile away. And yet David liked it—that was the strange thing. Once it had been new and strange and frightening. Now it was his home.

"Are your parents coming?" Jill asked.

"What?"

"In two weeks' time. For prize-giving."

David had hardly seen Edward and Eileen Eliot since the day he had started at Groosham Grange. Parents very rarely came to the school. But as it happened, he had received a letter from his father just a few days before:

Dear David,

This is to inform you that your mother and I will be visiting Groosham Grange for prize-giving on October 31. We will also be bringing my sister, your aunt Mildred, and will then drive her home to Margate. This means that I will be spending only half the day at the school. To save time, I am also sending you only half a letter.

And that was where it ended. The page had been torn neatly in two.

"Yes. They're coming," David said. "How about yours?"

"No." Jill shook her head. Her father was a diplomat and her mother an actress, so she hardly ever saw either of them. "Dad's in Argentina and Mom's acting in *The Cherry Orchard.*"

"Has she got a good part?"

"She's playing one of the cherries."

They had reached the school now. Jill glanced at her watch. "It's two minutes to four," she said. "We're going to be late."

"You go ahead," David muttered.

"Cheer up, David." Jill started forward, then turned her head. "You're probably right. You'll win the Grail. There's nothing to worry about."

David watched her go, then turned off, making his way around the East Tower and on through the school's own private cemetery. It was a shortcut he often used. But now, just as he reached the first grave, he stopped. Before he knew what he was doing, he had crouched down behind a gravestone, all other thoughts having emptied out of his head.

Slowly, he peered over the top. A door had opened at the side of the school. There was nothing strange about that except that the door was always locked. It led into a small antechamber in the East Tower. From there, a stone staircase spiraled more than five hundred feet up to a completely circular room at the top. Nobody ever went into the East Tower. There was nothing downstairs and the old, crumbling stairway was supposedly too

25

dangerous to climb. The whole place was off-limits. But somebody was about to come out. Who?

A few seconds later the question was answered as a boy stepped out, looking cautiously about him. David recognized him at once: his blond hair thrown back in a fancy wave across his forehead and his piercing blue eyes, which were now narrow and guarded. Vincent King had been up to something in the East Tower and he didn't want anyone to know about it. Without turning back, he pulled the door shut behind him, then hurried away in the direction of the school.

David waited a few moments before rising from behind the gravestone. He was going to be late for his French class and he knew it would get him into trouble, but his curiosity had gotten the better of him. What had Vincent been doing inside? He started forward. The tower rose up in front of him, half strangled by the ivy that twisted around it. He could just make out the slit of a window beneath the battlements. Was it just a trick of the light or was something moving behind it? Had Vincent been meeting someone high up in the circular room?

He reached out for the door.

But then a hand clamped down on his shoulder, spinning him around as somebody lurched at him, appearing from nowhere. David caught his breath. Then he relaxed. It was only Gregor, the school porter.

Even so, anyone else being stopped by such a creature on the edge of a cemetery would probably have had a heart attack. Gregor was like something out of a horror film, his neck broken and his skin like moldy cheese. At least the javelin had been removed from his back, although he evidently hadn't changed his shirt. David could still see the hole where the javelin had gone in.

"Vareyoo goink, young master?" Gregor asked in his strange, gurgling voice. Gregor chewed on his words like raw meat. He also chewed raw meat. His table manners were so disgusting that he was usually made to eat under the table.

"I was just . . ." David wasn't sure what to say.

"Butzee classes, young master. Yoom issink zee lovely classes. You shoot be hurrink in." Gregor moved so that he stood between David and the door to the tower.

"Hold on, Gregor," David began. "I just need a few minutes—"

"No minutes." Gregor lurched from one foot to the other, his hands hanging down to his knees. "Is bad marks for missink classes. And too many bad marks and there izno Unnerly Grail for the young master. Yes! Gregor knows . . ."

"What do you know, Gregor?" Suddenly David was suspicious. It was almost as if Gregor had been waiting for him at the tower. Had he seen Vincent coming out? And why had he suddenly mentioned the Grail? There was certainly more to this than met the eye . . . which, in Gregor's case, was about an inch below his other eye.

"Hurry, young master," Gregor insisted.

"All right," David said. "I'm going." He turned his back on the porter and walked quickly toward his classroom. But now he was certain. He had been listening to the voice of his sixth sense when he was down on the rocks—and hadn't Groosham Grange taught him that the sixth sense was much more important than the other five?

Something was going on at the school. In some way it was connected to the Unholy Grail. And whatever it was, David was going to find out.

David opened the classroom door nervously. He was ten minutes late, which was bad enough, but this was French with Monsieur Leloup, which was worse. Monsieur Leloup had a bad temper—hardly surprising considering he was a werewolf. Even on a good day he had been known to rip a French dictionary to pieces with his teeth. On a bad day, when there was going to be a full moon, he had to be chained to his desk in case he did the same to his class.

Fortunately, the full moon had come and gone, but even so, David walked gingerly into the room. His empty desk stared accusingly at him in the middle of all the others. Just as he reached it, Monsieur Leloup turned from the blackboard.

"You are late, Monsieur Eliot," he snapped.

"I'm sorry, sir . . ." David said.

"Ten minutes late. Can you tell me where you have been?"

David opened his mouth to speak, then thought better of it. He could see Vincent out of the corner of his eye. Vincent had the desk behind his. He was pretending to read his book, but there was a half smile on his lips, as if he knew what was going to happen. "I was just out walking," David said.

"Walking?" Monsieur Leloup sniffed. "I shall deduct three points from the standings list. Now will you please take your seat. We are discussing the future perfect . . ."

David sat down and opened his book. He had gotten off lightly and he knew it. Three points deducted still left him twenty-seven ahead. There was no way Vincent could catch up, no matter what happened in the last exam. He was fine.

Even so, David concentrated more than usual for the next fifty minutes just in case he was asked something, and he was relieved when the bell rang at five o'clock and the class was over.

He joined the general stream out of the class and down the corridor to the last lesson of the day. He found this one a lot more interesting: general witchcraft, taught by Mrs. Windergast. Even after a year at the school, David still hadn't quite gotten used to the matron's methods. Only a week before, he had gone to her with a headache and she had given him not an aspirin but an asp. She had fished the small, slithering snake out of a glass jar and held it against his head . . . an example of what she called sympathetic magic. David had found it a rather unnerving experience—although he'd been forced to admit that it worked.

Today she was discussing the power of flight. And she wasn't talking about airplanes.

"The broomstick was always the favored vehicle of the sisterhood," she was saying. "Can anyone tell me what it was made of?"

A girl in the front row put up her hand. "Hazelwood?"

"Quite right, Linda. Hazelwood is the correct answer. Now, who can tell me why some people believe that witches used to keep cats?"

The same girl put up her hand. "Because *cat* was the old word for broomstick," she volunteered.

"Right again, Linda." Mrs. Windergast muttered a few words. There was a flash of light, and with a little shriek, Linda exploded. All that was left of her was a puddle of slime and a few strands of hair. "It is never wise to know all the answers," Mrs. Windergast remarked acidly. "To answer once is fine. To answer twice is showing off. I hope Linda will have learned that now."

Mrs. Windergast smiled. She was a small, round woman who looked like the perfect grandmother. But in fact she was lethal. She had been burned at the stake in 1214 (during the reign of King John) and again in 1336. Not surprisingly, she now tended to keep herself to herself and she never went to barbecues.

"Linda was, however, quite right," she continued. She pulled a broomstick out from behind the blackboard. "Witches never had cats. It was just a misunderstanding. This is my own 'cat' and today I want to show you how difficult it is to control. Would anyone like to try it?"

Nobody moved. All eyes were on Linda's empty desk and the green smoke still curling above it.

Mrs. Windergast pointed. "Vincent King . . ."

Vincent stood up and moved to the front of the classroom. David's eyes narrowed. Mrs. Windergast was obviously in a bad mood today. Maybe Vincent would say something to annoy her and go the same way as Linda. Or was that too much to hope?

"My broomstick is very precious to me," Mrs. Windergast was saying. "I normally keep it very close to me—as do all witches. So this is very much an honor, young man. Do you think you could ride it?"

"Yeah—I think so."

"Then try."

Vincent took hold of the broomstick and muttered some words of power. At once the stick sprang to attention and hovered in the air, several feet above the ground. Gracefully, he climbed onto it, swinging one leg over it as if it were a horse. David watched, annoyed and showing it. It seemed there was nothing Vincent couldn't do well. He had both feet off the ground now, hovering in space as if he had been born to it.

"Try moving," Mrs. Windergast suggested.

Vincent concentrated and slowly rose into the air, perfectly balanced on the broomstick. Gently he curved round and headed over the blackboard, the handle ahead of him, the twigs trailing behind. He was smiling, growing in confidence, and David was half tempted to whisper the spell that would summon up a minor wind demon and knock him off balance.

But in the end there was no need. When things went wrong, they all went wrong at once. The broomstick wobbled, the end pitched up, Vincent cried out and the next moment he fell off and crashed to the floor with the broom on top of him.

"As you can see," Mrs. Windergast trilled, "it's not as easy as it looks. Is there any damage, Vincent dear?"

Vincent got stiffly to his feet, rubbing his shoulder. "I'm all right," he said.

"I meant the broomstick." Mrs. Windergast picked it up and cast a fond eye over it. "I never let anyone ride it as a rule," she went on. "But it seems undamaged. Well done, Vincent. You may return to your seat. And now"— she turned to the blackboard—"let me try to explain the curious mixture of magic and basic aerodynamics that makes flight possible."

For the next forty-five minutes, Mrs. Windergast explained her technique. David was sorry when the final bell went. He had enjoyed the lesson—Vincent's fall in particular—and he was still smiling as he left the classroom. Linda followed him out. She had been reconstituted by Mrs. Windergast, but she was looking very pale and sickly. David doubted if she would ever make a decent black magician. She'd probably end up as nothing worse than a crossing guard.

There was a knot of people outside in the corridor. As David came out he saw that one of them was Vincent.

"That was bad luck," Vincent said.

"What?" Maybe it was just an innocent remark, but already David felt his hackles rise.

"Losing three points in French. That narrows the gap."

"You're still a long way behind." It was Jill who had spoken. David hadn't seen her arrive, but he was glad that she seemed to have taken his side.

"The exams aren't over yet." Vincent shrugged and once again David was irritated without knowing why. Did he dislike Vincent just because he was his closest rival or was there something more? Looking at his easy smile, the way Vincent slouched against the wall—always so superior—he felt something snap inside.

"You looked pretty stupid just now," he said.

"When?"

"Falling off the broomstick."

"You think you could have done better?"

"Sure." David wasn't thinking. All he knew was that he wanted to goad the other boy, just to get a reaction. "You're going to have to get used to coming in second," he went on. "Just like in the race . . ."

Vincent's eyes narrowed. He took a step forward. "There was only one reason I came in second . . ." he began.

He knew what David had done. He had felt the web slipping over his foot. And he was going to say it, now, in front of everyone. David couldn't let that happen. He had to stop him. And before he knew what he was doing, he suddenly reached out and pushed Vincent hard with the heel of his hand. Vincent was caught off balance and cried out as his bruised shoulder hit the wall behind him.

"David!" Jill cried out.

She was too late. Without hesitating, Vincent bounced back, throwing himself onto David. David's books and papers were torn out of his hands and scattered across the floor. Vincent was taller, heavier and stronger than David. But even as he felt the other boy's hand on his throat, he couldn't help feeling pleased with himself. He had wanted to get past Vincent's defenses and he'd done it. He'd taken the upper hand.

Right now, though, Vincent's upper hand was slowly strangling him. David brought up his knee, felt it sink into Vincent's stomach. Vincent grunted and twisted hard. David's head cracked against the paneling.

"What's going on here? Stop it at once!"

David's heart sank. Of all the people who could have happened along the corridor just then, Mr. Helliwell was unquestionably the worst. He was a huge man with wide shoulders and a round, bald head. He had only recently joined the school, teaching arts and crafts by day and voodoo by night. He came from Haiti, where he was apparently so feared as a magician that people actually fainted if he said "good morning" to them and for six months the postman had been too scared to deliver the mail—which didn't matter too much as nobody on the island was brave enough to write. David had somehow found himself on the wrong side of Mr. Helliwell from the very start and this was only going to make things worse.

"David? Vincent?" The teacher looked from one to the other. "Who started this?"

David hesitated. He was blushing and it was only now that he realized how stupid he had been. He had behaved like an ordinary boy at an ordinary school. At

Groosham Grange, there was no worse crime. "It was me," he admitted.

Vincent looked at him but said nothing. Jill and the other onlookers seemed to have vanished. There were just the three of them left in the corridor. Mr. Helliwell glanced down at the floor. He leaned forward, picked up a sheet of paper and quickly read it. He handed it to David. "This is yours."

David took it. It was the letter from his father.

"You started the fight?" Mr. Helliwell asked.

"Yes," David said.

Mr. Helliwell considered. His gray eyes gave nothing away. "Very well," he said. "This is going to cost you nine points. And if I see you behaving like this again, I'll send you to the heads."

Mr. Helliwell turned and walked away. David watched him go, then leaned down and picked up the rest of his books and papers. He could feel Vincent watching him. He glanced up.

Vincent shrugged. "Don't blame me," he said.

And then he was on his own. In one afternoon he had lost an incredible twelve points! His lead had gone down by almost half—from thirty to eighteen. At lunchtime he had been right at the top of the standings list, secure, unassailable. But now . . .

David gritted his teeth. There was only one more exam to go. It was his best subject. And he was still a long way ahead of Vincent. The Unholy Grail would be his.

Scooping up the last of his books, David set off down the empty corridor, the sound of his own footsteps echoing around him.

Framed

Canterbury
Cathedral

Sports Day

Flying Lesson

Vincent

Departure

Wax

Cracks

Needle in
a Haystack

Pursuit

The Exam

On the Rocks

The East
Tower

Prize-Giving

That night David had a bad dream.

Vincent King was part of it, of course. Vincent laughing at him. Vincent holding the Unholy Grail. Vincent slipping out of the East Tower and disappearing like a wisp of smoke into one of the graves.

But there were other, more frightening things woven into the night canvas. First there were his parents—only they weren't his parents. They were changing, transforming into something horrible. And then there was a face that he knew, looming over him. He would have been able to recognize it, but he was lying on his back, in pain, blinded by a fiery sun. And finally he saw the school, Groosham Grange, standing stark against a darkening sky. As he watched, a bolt of lightning streaked down and smashed into it. A great crack appeared in the stonework. Dust and rubble exploded out.

And that was when he woke up.

There were nine dormitories at Groosham Grange. The one that David slept in was completely circular, with the beds arranged like numbers on a clock face. Vincent had been put in the same room as him, his bed opposite David's, underneath a window. Propping himself up on one elbow, David could see the other boy's bed, clearly illuminated by a shaft of moonlight flooding in from above. It was empty.

Where could Vincent be? David glanced at the chair beside Vincent's bed. Wherever he had gone, he had taken his clothes with him. Outside, a clock struck four. At almost exactly the same moment, David heard a door creak open somewhere below and then swing shut. It had to be Vincent. Nobody else would be up and about in the middle of the night. David threw back the covers and got out of bed. He would find out what was going on.

He got dressed quickly and crept out of the room. There had been a time when he would have been afraid to wander through the empty school in the darkness, but the night no longer held any fear for him. And he knew the building with its twisting corridors and sudden, plunging staircases so well that he didn't even need to carry a flashlight.

With the wooden stairs creaking beneath his feet, he made his way to the ground floor. Which door had he heard open and close? Ahead of him, the main entrance to the school rose up about thirty feet, a great wall of oak studded with iron. The door was bolted securely from inside so Vincent couldn't have passed through there. Behind him, going back underneath the staircase, a second door led into the Great Hall, where meals were served.

This door was open but the room behind it was shrouded in darkness and silent but for the flutter of the bats that lived high up in the rafters.

David reached the bottom of the staircase and stood silently on the cold, marble floor. He was surrounded by oil paintings, portraits of former heads and teachers—a true collection of old masters. All of them seemed to be looking at him, and as he moved forward the eyes swiveled to follow him and he heard a strange, musty whispering as the pictures muttered to one another.

"Where's he going? What's he doing?"

"He's making a mistake!"

"Don't do it, David."

"Go back to bed, David."

David ignored them. To one side a passage stretched out into the darkness, blocked at the end by a door he knew led into the library. There were two more doors facing each other halfway along the passage. The one on the left led into the office of Mr. Kilgraw, the assistant headmaster. As usual it was closed and no light showed through the crack. But on the other side of the passageway . . . David felt the hairs on the back of his neck tingle. A square of light stretched out underneath the door. This one was marked HEADS. The room behind it belonged, of course, to Mr. Fitch and Mr. Teagle.

David was certain they weren't in their study. Only that afternoon they had complained of the very worst thing they could possibly get—a headache—and had announced they were going to bed early. Mr. Fitch and Mr. Teagle had no choice but to sleep in the same bed (though with two pillows) and rather curiously both men talked in their sleep, often having animated conversations right through the night.

But if Vincent was behind the door, what was he doing

there? Going as quietly as he could—even the slightest movement seemed to echo throughout the school—David tiptoed along the corridor. Slowly, he reached out for the handle, his hand throwing an elongated shadow across the door. He hadn't even worked out what he would do when he discovered Vincent. But that didn't matter. He just wanted to see him.

He opened the door and blinked. The room was empty.

Closing the door behind him, David entered the heads' inner sanctum. The room was more like a chapel than a study, with its black marble floor and stained-glass windows. The furniture was solid and heavy, the desk a great block of wood that could have been an altar. Leather-bound books lined the walls, the shelves sagging under their weight. David knew he would be in serious trouble if he was found here. Nobody was allowed in this room unless summoned. But it was too late to turn back now.

The light that he had seen came from a lamp on a chest of drawers that stretched the whole length of the room. David ran his eyes along the surface, past a tangle of test tubes and pipes, a stuffed rat, a human skull, a computer, a pair of thumbscrews and a German helmet from the First World War. He was puzzled. What, he wondered, was the computer for?

But this was no time to ask questions. Vincent wasn't in the room. That was all that mattered. *He* shouldn't be here either. He had to go.

It was as he turned to leave that he saw it. There was a small table in the far corner with a circular hole in the wall just above it. A picture lay faceup on the carpet nearby. A safe! Somebody had taken down the picture and opened the safe. Like a moth to a flame he moved toward the table. There were four sheets of paper lying on the top. David knew what they were even before he reached out and picked them up. He looked down at the front cover.

GROOSHAM GRANGE EXAMINING BOARD
General Certificate of Secondary Education
ADVANCED CURSING

He was standing beside the open safe, holding the exam papers, when the door crashed open behind him. With a dreadful lurching feeling in his stomach, he looked round, knowing that he had been set up, knowing that it was too late to do anything about it. Mr. Fitch and Mr. Teagle were there, wearing a bathrobe and pajamas. With them (and this was the only surprise) was Mr. Helliwell. He was fully dressed. All three men—or all two and a half—were gazing at him in disbelief.

"David . . . !" Mr. Fitch exclaimed. His long, hooked nose curved toward David accusingly.

"What are you doing here?" Mr. Teagle demanded. He was wearing a nightcap with a pom-pom dangling just next to his chin. He shook his head disapprovingly and the pom-pom swung back and forth as if in agreement.

"I never thought it would be you, David," Mr. Helliwell said. The voodoo teacher looked genuinely astonished—and sad. He turned to the heads. "I heard someone go into your office," he explained. "But I never dreamed . . ."

"You were quite right to come to us, Mr. Helliwell," Mr. Fitch said.

"Quite right," Mr. Teagle agreed.

"You can leave us now," Mr. Fitch continued. "We'll take care of this."

Mr. Helliwell paused as if he was about to say something. He glanced at David and shook his head. Then, with a quiet "good night," he turned and left the room.

Mr. Fitch and Mr. Teagle remained where they were.

"Do you have anything to say for yourself, David?" Mr. Teagle asked.

David thought for a moment. The bitterness of his defeat was in his mouth and he wanted to spit it out. But he knew when he was beaten. Somehow he had been lured into a trap. The portraits had tried to warn him, but he hadn't listened and now it was too late to talk himself out of it. What could he say? The safe was open. The exam papers were in his hand. There was nobody else in the room. Trying to explain would only make matters worse.

He shook his head.

"Really, I am very disappointed in you," Mr. Fitch said.

"And I am disappointed too." Mr. Teagle stroked his beard. "It's not just that you were cheating. That would be bad enough."

"But you were *caught* cheating," Mr. Fitch continued. "That's even worse. How could you be so clumsy? So amateurish?"

"And why did you even bother?" Mr. Teagle asked. "You would easily have come first in Advanced Cursing without stealing the papers. Now we'll have to change all the questions. Completely rewrite the exam . . ."

"The exam is on Wednesday." Mr. Fitch sighed. "That only gives us two days."

"We have no choice." Mr. Teagle said. "We'll have to start again." He turned to David. "You won't believe this," he went on, "but writing exams is almost as boring as taking them! It's all most annoying."

Both men nodded at the same time, narrowly missing banging their heads together. Still David said nothing. He was furious with himself. He had walked into this. How could he have been so stupid?

"Are you aware of the seriousness of this offense?" Mr. Teagle asked.

David was blushing darkly. He couldn't keep silent any longer. "It's not the way it looks," he said. "It's not what you think—"

"Oh no," Mr. Fitch interrupted. "I suppose you're going to tell us that you were framed."

"Maybe you didn't mean to come in here and look at the exams," Mr. Teagle suggested sarcastically.

David hung his head low. "No," he whispered.

"You realize that we could expel you for this," Mr. Fitch said.

"Or worse," Mr. Teagle agreed.

Mr. Fitch sighed. "Sometimes I wonder, David, if you're suited to Groosham Grange. When you first came here, you fought against us. In a way you're still fighting. Do you really think you belong here?"

Did he belong at Groosham Grange? It was something that, in his darker moments, he had often wondered.

When he had first come to the school, he had indeed fought against it. As soon as he had learned about the secret lessons in black magic, he had done everything he could to escape, to tell the authorities what he knew, to get the place closed down. It had only been when he had found himself trapped and helpless that he had changed his mind. If you can't beat them . . .

But here he was, a year later, determined to become the number one student, to win the Unholy Grail. He remembered the fear he had once felt, the sense of horror. Classes in black magic! Ghosts and vampires! Now he was one of them—so what exactly did that make him? What had he become in the year he had been here?

He became aware of the heads, waiting for an answer.

"I do belong here," he said. "I know that now. But . . ." He hesitated. "I'm not evil."

"Evil?" Mr. Teagle smiled for the first time. "What is good and what is evil?" he asked. "Sometimes it's not as easy as you think to tell them apart. That's still something you have to learn."

David nodded. "Maybe that's true," he said. "But all I know is . . . this is my home. And I do want to stay."

"Very well." Mr. Fitch was suddenly businesslike. "We won't expel you. But tonight's performance is going to cost you ten points—"

"Fifteen," Mr. Teagle cut in.

"Fifteen points. Do you have anything to say?"

David shook his head. He was feeling sick to the stomach. Fifteen points! Add that to the twelve points he had lost earlier in the day and that left . . .

"David?"

. . . just three points. Three points between Vincent and him. How had it happened? How had Vincent managed to lure him here?

"No, sir." His voice was hoarse, a whisper.

"Then I suggest you go back to bed."

"Yes . . ."

David was still holding the exam papers. Clenching

his teeth, feeling the bitterness rising inside him, he jerked his fingers open, dropping them back onto the table. He hadn't read a single question.

He left the study and walked back along the passage and past the portraits, trying to ignore them tut-tutting at him as he went. With his mind still spinning, he climbed the stairs and found his way back to the dormitory. He stopped by his bed. Vincent was back. His clothes were on the chair, his body curled up under the blankets as if he had never been away. But was he really asleep? David gazed through the darkness at the half smile on the other boy's face and doubted it.

Silently, David undressed again and got back into bed. Three points. That was all there was between them. Over and over again he muttered the figure to himself until at last he fell into an angry, restless sleep.

The Exam

Wednesday quickly came, and with it the last examination of the year: Advanced Cursing.

There was a tradition at Groosham Grange that all the ordinary exams were taken upstairs, in the Great Hall. But for the more secretive ones, the exams relating to witchcraft and black magic, the pupils went downstairs through the network of tunnels and secret passages that lay beneath the school and into an underground chamber where sixty-five desks and sixty-five chairs had been set up, far away from the prying sun. This, then, was to be the final testing ground: a hidden cavern among the stalactites and stalagmites with a great waterfall of crystallized rock guarding the way out.

The exam was to start at eleven o'clock. At a quarter to, David made his way downstairs. His mouth was dry and he had an unpleasant feeling in the pit of his stomach. It was crazy. When it came to Advanced Cursing, everyone agreed he was untouchable. At the same time, he knew that it was one of Vincent's weakest subjects. That morning he had checked the standings list one last time. He was still in first place. Vincent was three points behind. After that there was a gap of seventeen points to Jill, who was in third place. Looking at the bulletin board had told him what he wanted to know. This exam was between him and Vincent. And Vincent didn't have a chance.

So why was he feeling so nervous? David opened the door of the library and went in. Ahead of him there was a full-length mirror and he glanced at his reflection while he walked toward it. He was tired and it showed. He hadn't slept well since his encounter in the heads' study. He was still having the dreams: his parents, the school breaking up and the face that he was sure he recognized.

He was right up against his reflection now. He scowled at himself briefly, then walked into the glass. The mirror rippled around him like water and then he had passed

through it and into the first of the underground passages. His breath steamed slightly in the cold air as he
followed the path down and he could feel the moisture
clinging to his clothes. The examination room lay straight
ahead, but on an impulse David took a fork, following a
second passageway to the right. This was no more than
a fissure in the rock, so narrow in places that he had to
hold his breath to squeeze through. But then it widened
out again and David found himself face to face with what
he had come to see.

The Unholy Grail was kept in a miniature grotto, separated from the passageway by six iron bars. The bars
were embedded in the rock, and there was no visible
way through to the chamber behind. The Grail stood on
a rock pedestal, bathed in an unnatural silver light. It
was about six inches high, a metallic gray in color, en-
crusted with dark red stones that were either rubies or
carbuncles. There was nothing very extraordinary about
it to look at. But David found that his breath had caught
in his throat. He was hypnotized by it. He could sense
the power that the Grail contained and he would have
given anything to reach through the bars and hold it in
his hand.

This was what he was fighting for. He would take

the exam and he would come in first. Nobody would stop him.

"David . . . ?"

Hearing his name, David swung around guiltily. He had been so absorbed in the Grail that he hadn't heard anyone approach. He turned and saw the arts, crafts and voodoo master, Mr. Helliwell, standing at the entrance. He was wearing a dark, three-piece suit. It was the old-fashioned sort and made him look like a funeral director. "What are you doing here?" he asked.

"I was just looking . . ." David was being defensive. After their meeting two nights before, he had nothing more to say. But to his surprise Mr. Helliwell moved closer and there was a frown of puzzlement on his face. "David," he began. "I want to talk to you about the other night."

"What about it?" David knew he was being deliberately rude, but he was still angry about what had happened.

Mr. Helliwell sighed. The light was reflecting off the huge dome of his head and his round, gray eyes seemed troubled. "I know you're upset," he said. "But there's something I have to tell you. I don't believe it was you who opened the safe."

"What?" David felt a surge of excitement.

"I was as surprised as anyone to find you in that room," the teacher went on. "Let me explain. I was making my rounds when I saw someone come down the stairs. It was dark, so I didn't see who it was. But I could have sworn they had fair hair, lighter than yours."

Fair hair. That was Vincent. It had to be.

"I saw them go into the heads' study, and that was when I went to get Mr. Fitch and Mr. Teagle." Mr. Helliwell paused. "Whoever was inside the study had left the door half open. I'd swear to that. Only, when we got back the door was closed. And *you* were inside."

"I didn't open the safe," David said. Now that he had started, he couldn't stop. "Someone set me up. They wanted me to be found there. They knew you'd gone for the heads. And they must have slipped out just before I arrived."

"Someone . . . ?" Mr. Helliwell frowned. "Do you have any idea who?"

For a moment David was tempted to name Vincent King. But that wasn't the way he did things. He shook his head. "Why didn't you tell the heads what you'd seen?" he asked.

Mr. Helliwell shrugged. "At the time it seemed

an open-and-shut case. It was only afterward . . ." He stroked his chin. "Even now I'm not sure. I suppose I believe you. But it's your word against . . ."

. . . against Vincent's. David nodded. The trap had been too well prepared.

Mr. Helliwell pulled a pocket watch from his waistcoat pocket and looked at it. "It's almost eleven o'clock," he said. He reached out and put a firm, heavy hand on David's shoulder. "But if you have any more problems, you come to me. Maybe I can help."

"Thank you." David turned and hurried back down the passageway. He was feeling ten times more confident than an hour before. He had let Vincent beat him once. There wouldn't be a second time.

He would take the exam and he would come in first. And the Unholy Grail would be his.

GROOSHAM GRANGE EXAMINING BOARD
General Certificate of Secondary Education
ADVANCED CURSING
Wednesday, October 24, 11 a.m.
TIME: 2 hours
Write your name and candidate number in ink (not in blood) on each side of the paper. Write on

one side of the paper only, preferably not the thin side.

Answer all the questions. Each question is to be answered on a separate sheet.

The number of points available is shown in brackets at the end of each question or part question. The total for this paper is 100 points.

Candidates are warned not to attempt to curse the person who wrote this exam.

1. Write out in full the words of power that would cause the following curses (30):

a) Baldness (5)

b) Acne (5)

c) Bad breath (5)

d) Amnesia (5)

e) Death (10)

CAUTION: Do not mutter the words of power as you write them. If anyone near you loses their hair, breaks out in pimples, smells like an onion, forgets why they're here and/or dies, you will be disqualified.

2. Your aunt announces that she has come to stay for Christmas and New Year.

She is seventy years old and leaves a lipstick

65

mark on your cheek when she kisses you. Although you are fifteen, she still insists that you are nine. She criticizes your clothes, your hair and your taste in music. As usual, she has brought you a book token.

Describe in two hundred words a suitable curse that would ensure she spends next Christmas in (10):

a) The intensive-care unit of your local hospital OR

b) A rice field in China OR

c) A crater on the dark side of the moon

3. What is thanatomania? Define it, giving two historical examples. Then describe how you would survive it. (35)

4. Write down a suitable curse for THREE of the following people (15):

a) Elephant poachers (5)

b) People who talk during movies (5)

c) Litterbugs (5)

d) Cigarette manufacturers (5)

e) Bullies (5)

5. Describe how you would re-create the Great

Plague using ingredients found in your local supermarket. (10)

It was as easy as that.

As soon as David had run his eyes over the questions,
he knew he was going to be all right. He had even re-
viewed the Great Plague a few nights before and the rest
of the exam was just as straightforward.

So he was smiling when the clock struck one and Mr.
Helliwell called time. While everyone else remained in
their seats, Vincent and another boy who had been sitting in the front row got up and started collecting the
papers. It was Vincent who came over to David's desk.
As he handed his answers over, David lifted his head and
allowed his eyes to lock with Vincent's. He didn't say
anything, but he wanted the other boy to know. *I got
every question right. Nothing can stop me now.*

Mr. Helliwell dropped the papers into his leather bag
and everyone was allowed to leave. Once they were back
out in the open air, David caught up with Jill. It was a
beautiful afternoon. The sun felt warm on his neck after
the chill of the cave.

"How did it go?" he asked.

Jill grimaced. "Awful. What on earth is thinato-mania?"

"Thanatomania. It's a sort of multiple curse," David explained. "It was when a witch wanted to hurt a whole town or village instead of just one person." He shuddered. "I don't know why they teach us about things like that. It's not as if we'd ever want to curse anyone."

"No," Jill agreed. "But most of the stuff you learn at school you never actually use. You just have to know about it, that's all." She took his arm. "So how did you do?"

David smiled. "It was easy."

"I'm glad you think so." Jill looked away. In the distance, Vincent was walking off on his own toward the East Tower. He was smiling and there was a spring in his step. "I wouldn't count your chickens too soon," she said. "There goes Vincent. And he looks pretty confident too."

David remembered her words over the next few days. There were more classes, but with the final exam over, the standings list was officially closed. Everything now hinged on Advanced Cursing, and although David was sure of himself, although he pretended he wasn't thinking about it, he still found himself hanging around the bulletin board near the heads' study where the results would eventually be posted.

And he was there one evening when Mr. Kilgraw, the assistant headmaster, appeared, a sheet of paper in one hand and a thumbtack in the other. David felt his heartbeat quicken. There was a lump in his throat and a tingling in the palms of his hands. Nobody else was around. He would be the first to know the results.

Forcing himself not to run, he went over to the bulletin board. Mr. Kilgraw gave him a deathly smile. "Good evening, David."

"Good evening, sir." Why didn't Mr. Kilgraw say anything? Why didn't he congratulate David on coming in first, on winning the Unholy Grail? With difficulty, he forced his eyes up to take in the bulletin board. And there it was:

ADVANCED CURSING—RESULTS

But the name on the top was not his own.

Linda James, the girl who had been disintegrated by Mrs. Windergast, was first.

David blinked. What about the name underneath her?

William Rufus had come in second.

Then Jeffrey Joseph.

It wasn't possible.

"A very disappointing result for you, David." Mr. Kilgraw was talking, but David hardly heard him. He was panicking now. The typed letters on the list were blurring into one another as he searched through them for his name. There was Vincent, in ninth place with sixty-eight points. And there he was, two places below . . . eleventh! He had scored only sixty-five. It was impossible!

"Very disappointing," Mr. Kilgraw said, but there was something strange in his voice. It was as soft and as menacing as ever, but there was something else. Was he pleased?

Eleventh . . . David felt numb. He tried to work out where it left him on the standings list. Linda had scored seventy-six points. He was eleven behind her, three behind Vincent. He had lost the Grail. He must have.

"I was quite surprised," Mr. Kilgraw went on. "I would have thought you would have known the meaning of *thanatomania*."

"Thanato . . . ?" David's voice seemed to be coming from a long way away. He turned to Mr. Kilgraw. He could hear footsteps approaching. News had gotten out that the results were there. Soon there would be a crowd. "But I *do* know," David said. "I wrote it down . . ."

Mr. Kilgraw shook his head with a sad smile. "I marked the papers myself," he said. "You didn't even tackle the question."

"But . . . I did! I got it right!"

"No, David. It was Question Three. I must say, you got everything else right. But I'm afraid you lost thirty-five points on that one. You didn't hand in an answer."

Hand in an answer . . .

And then David remembered. Vincent had collected the papers. He had handed them to Vincent. And following the instructions at the top of the exam, each question had been answered on a separate sheet. It would have been simple for Vincent to slip one of the pages out. David had been so confident, so sure of himself, that he hadn't even thought of it. But that must have been what had happened. That was the only possibility.

There were about twenty or thirty people milling around the bulletin board now, struggling to get closer, calling out names and numbers. David heard his own name called out. Eleventh with sixty-five points.

"That means he's tied for first," somebody shouted. "He and Vincent King are tied for first."

"So who gets the Unholy Grail?"

Everybody was chattering around him. Feeling sick and confused, David pushed his way through the crowd and ran off, ignoring Jill and the others who were calling after him.

There was no moon that night. As if to add to the darkness, a mist had rolled in from the sea, slithering over the damp earth and curling up against the walls of Groosham Grange. Everything was silent. Even Gregor—sound asleep on one of the tombstones in the cemetery—was actually making no sound. Normally he snored. Tonight he was still.

Nobody heard the door creak open to one side of the school. Nobody saw a figure step out into the night and make its way over the moss and the soil toward the East Tower. A second door opened and closed. Inside the tower, a light flickered on.

But nobody saw the lantern as it turned around and around on itself, being carried ever higher up the spiral staircase that led to the battlements. A bloated spider scuttled out of the way, just managing to avoid the heel of a black leather shoe that pounded down on the concrete step. A rat arched its back in a corner, fearful of the unaccustomed light. But no human eye was open. No human ear heard the thud, thud, thud of footsteps climbing the stairs.

The secret agent reached a circular room at the top of the tower, its eight narrow windows open to the night. To one side there was a table, some paper and what looked like a collection of boxes. From inside the boxes came the sound of flapping and a strange, high-pitched squeak. The agent sat down and drew one of the sheets of paper forward. And began to write:

TOP SECRET
To the Bishop of Bletchley
All is going according to plan. Nobody suspects. Very soon the Unholy Grail will be ours.
Expect further news soon.

Once again there was no signature at the bottom of the page. The agent scrawled a single *X*, then folded the letter carefully and reached into one of the boxes. It wasn't actually a box but a cage. His hand came out again holding something that looked like a scrap of torn leather except that it was alive, jerking and squealing. The agent attached the message to the creature's leg, then carried it over to the window.

"Off you go." The words were a soft whisper in the darkness.

A brief flurry. A last cry. And then the message was gone, carried off into the swirling night.

Framed

Canterbury Cathedral

Sports Day

Flying Lesson

Vincent

Departure

Wax

Cracks

Needle in a Haystack

Pursuit

The Exam

On the Rocks

The East Tower

Prize Giving

It's a very unusual situation," Mr. Fitch said. "We have a tie."

"David Eliot and Vincent King," Mr. Teagle agreed. "Both have six hundred and sixty-six points."

"It's a bit of a nuisance," Mr. Fitch remarked peevishly. What are we going to do?"

Both men—or rather, both heads—looked around the table. The two of them were in the staff room, sitting in a single, high-backed chair. It was midday. Arranged around the table in front of them were Mr. Kilgraw, Mr. Helliwell, Mr. Creer, Mrs. Windergast, Monsieur Leloup and the oldest teacher in the school (by several centuries), Miss Pedicure. Miss Pedicure taught English, although at the start of her career this had been a bit of a problem as English hadn't been invented. She was now so frail and wrinkled that everyone would stop and stare whenever she sneezed, afraid that the effort might cause her to disintegrate.

Mr. Kilgraw grimaced, for a moment revealing two razor-sharp vampire teeth. There was a glass of red liquid on the table in front of him that might have been wine, but probably wasn't. "Is it not a tradition," he inquired, "in this circumstance to set some sort of trial? A tiebreaker?"

"What sort of trial do you have in mind?" Mrs. Windergast asked.

Mr. Kilgraw waved a languid hand. Because it was the middle of the day, the curtains in the room had been drawn for him, but enough of the light was filtering through to make him even paler than usual. "It will have to take place off the island," he said. "I would suggest London."

"Why London?" Miss Pedicure demanded.

"London is the capital," Mr. Kilgraw replied. "It is polluted, overcrowded and dangerous. A perfect arena—"

"Here, here!" Mrs. Windergast muttered.

"You agree?" Mr. Kilgraw asked.

"No. I was saying that the trial ought to take place here, here . . . on the island."

"No." Mr. Fitch rapped his knuckles on the table. "It's better if we send them out. More challenging."

"I have an idea," Mr. Kilgraw said.

"Do tell us," Mr. Fitch gurgled.

"Over the last year we have tested these boys in every aspect of the magical arts," Mr. Kilgraw began. "Cursing, levitation, shape-shifting, thanatomania—"

"What's thanatomania?" Mr. Creer demanded.

Mr. Kilgraw ignored him. "I suggest we set them a puzzle," he went on. "It will be a trial of skill and of the imagination. A meeting of two minds. It will take me a day or two to work out the details. But at least it will be final. Whoever wins the contest comes out top of the line and takes the Unholy Grail."

Everyone around the table murmured their assent. Mr. Fitch glanced at Mr. Helliwell. "Does it seem fair to you, Mr. Helliwell?" he asked.

The voodoo master nodded gravely. "I think that David Eliot deserves the Grail," he said. "If you ask me, there's something funny about the way he's lost so many points in such a short time. But this will give him a chance to prove himself. I'm sure he'll win. So I agree."

"Then it's decided," Mr. Teagle concluded. "Mr. Kilgraw will work on the tiebreaker. And perhaps you'll let me know when you've set something up."

Two days later, David and Vincent stood in one of the underground caverns of Skrull Island. They were both dressed casually in jeans and black, open-neck shirts. Mr. Kilgraw, Mr. Helliwell and Miss Pedicure were standing opposite them. At the back of the cave were two glass boxes that could have been shower cubicles except that they were empty. The boxes looked slightly ridiculous in the gloomy setting of the cave—like two theatrical props that had wandered offstage. But David knew what they were. One was for Vincent. The other was for him.

"You are to look for a needle in a haystack," Mr. Kilgraw was saying. "Some needles are bigger than others—and that may point you in the right direction. But the needle in question is a small statue of Miss Pedicure. I will tell you only that it is blue in color and two and a half inches high."

"It was taken from my mummy some years ago," Miss Pedicure sniffed. "I've always wanted to have it back."

"As for the haystack," Mr. Kilgraw went on, "that is the British Museum in London. All I will tell you is that the statue is somewhere inside. You have until midnight to find it. And there is one rule . . ." He nodded at Mr. Helliwell.

"You are not to use any magical powers," the voodoo teacher said. "We want this to be a test of stealth and cunning. We have helped you boys a little. We have arranged for the alarm system at the museum to turn itself off tonight and we have opened one door. But there will still be guards on duty. If you're caught, that's your own problem."

"It's seven o'clock now," Mr. Kilgraw said. "You have just five hours. Do you both understand what you have to do?"

David and Vincent nodded.

"Then let us begin. Whichever of you finds the statuette first and brings it back to this room will be declared the winner and will be awarded the Unholy Grail."

David glanced at Vincent. The two of them hadn't spoken to each other since the results of the exam had been announced. The tension between them almost crackled like static electricity. Vincent swept a blond lock of hair off his face. "I'll be waiting for you when you get back," he said.

"I'll be back here first," David replied.

They stepped into the boxes.

"Let the tiebreaker begin," Mr. Kilgraw commanded.

David felt the air inside the box go suddenly cold. He had been standing with his hands pressed against the glass, looking at Mr. Kilgraw. Then, slowly at first but accelerating quickly, the glass box began to turn. It was like an amusement-park ride except that there was no music, no sound at all, and he didn't feel nauseous or giddy. Mr. Kilgraw spun past him, a blur of color that had lost all sense of shape, blending in with the walls of the cave as the box turned faster and faster. Now the whole world had dissolved into a wheel of silver and gray. Then the lights went out.

David closed his eyes. When he opened them a moment later, he found he was looking at a street and a hedge. Swallowing, he pulled his hands away from the glass, leaving two damp palm prints behind. The box was illuminated from above by a single yellow bulb. A car drove past along the street, its headlights on.

David twisted around. Something bumped against his shoulder.

He was in a telephone booth. Not a modern kiosk but one of the old red telephone booths with a swinging door that stood in the middle of Regent's Park, London. It took him a moment to open it, but then he was standing on the pavement, breathing the night air. There was no sign of Vincent. He looked at his watch. Seven o'clock. He had traveled a hundred and twenty-five miles in less than a second.

But he was still a long way from the museum. Vincent would already be on his way. And this was his last chance . . .

David crossed the road and broke into a run.

In fact he took a taxi to the museum. He caught one in Baker Street and ordered the driver to go as fast as possible.

"The British Museum? You must be joking, buddy! There's no point going there now. It's closed for the night. Anyway, aren't you a bit young to be out on your own? You got any money?"

David had no money. Neither of the boys had been

given any—it was part of the test. Quickly, he hypnotized the driver. He knew he wasn't allowed to use magic, but Mr. Kilgraw had often told him that hypnosis was a science and not a magical power, so he decided it wouldn't count.

"The British Museum," he insisted. "And put your foot on it."

"Foot on it? All right, pal. Whatever you say. You're the boss." The driver shot through a red light, zigzagged across a busy intersection with cars hooting at him on all sides and accelerated the wrong way down a one-way street. The journey took them about ten minutes and David was relieved to get out.

He paid the driver with a leaf and two pebbles he had picked up in the park. "Keep the change," he said.

"Wow! Thanks, buddy." The cabdriver's eyes were still spinning. David watched him as he drove off across the sidewalk and into a store window, then slipped through the open gates of the British Museum.

But why were the gates open?

Had Mr. Helliwell arranged it for him? Or had Vincent gotten there first?

Feeling very small and vulnerable, David crossed the open space in front of the museum. The building itself was huge, bigger than he remembered. He had once heard that there were more than two miles of galleries inside, and looking at it now, its classical pillars arranged in two wings around a vast, central chamber, he could well believe it. His feet clattered faintly across the concrete as he ran forward. A well-mowed lawn, gray in the moonlight, stretched out as flat as paper on either side of him. There was a guardhouse next to the gate, but it was deserted. His shadow raced ahead of him, snaking up the steps as if trying to get into the building before him.

The main entrance to the museum was locked. For a moment David was tempted. A single spell would open the door. He could simply move the tumblers inside the lock with the power of thought or else he could turn himself into smoke and creep in through the crack underneath. But Mr. Helliwell had said *no magic*. And this time David was determined not to cheat. He would play by the rules.

It took him ten minutes to locate the side door that Mr. Kilgraw had opened. He slipped through and found himself standing on a stone floor beneath a ceiling that was so far above him that, in the half-light, he could barely see it. Doors led off to the left and right. Straight ahead there was an information desk and what looked like a souvenir shop. A grand staircase guarded by two stone lions swept up to one side. Which way should he go?

It was only now that he was here that David grasped the enormity of the task that faced him. Miss Pedicure had lived for three thousand years. And she had lived in just about every part of the world. So this statue of her—which had once belonged to her mother—could come from anywhere and any time. It was two and a half inches high and it was blue. That was all he knew.

So much for the needle. But what about the haystack?

The British Museum was enormous. How many exhibits did it hold? Ten thousand? A hundred thousand? Some of them were the size of small buildings. Some of them, in fact, *were* small buildings. Others were no bigger than a pin. The museum held collections from Ancient Greece, Ancient Egypt, Babylon, Persia, China; from the Iron Age, the Bronze Age, the Middle Ages, every age. There were tools and pottery, clocks and jewelry, masks and ivory . . . He could spend a year in the place and still get nowhere close.

David heard the rattle of a chain and pressed himself

back against the wall, well into the shadows. A guard appeared, walking down the stairs and into the main hall. He was dressed in blue pants and a white shirt, with a bunch of keys dangling from his waist. He paused in the middle of the entrance hall, yawned and stretched his arms, then disappeared behind the information desk.

Crouching in the dark, David considered. As far as he could see, he had two choices. One: search the museum as quickly as he could and hope for a lucky break. Two: look for some sort of catalog and try to find the statuette listed there. But even if a catalog existed, how would he know what to look for? It was hardly likely that Miss Pedicure's name would turn up in the index and there were probably statuettes in just about every room in the building.

That left only the first option. Straightening up again, David crossed the hall and climbed the staircase that the guard had just come down. He would have to hope for a little luck.

Three and a half hours later he was back where he'd started.

His head was pounding and his eyes were sore with

fatigue. The stairs had led him up past a Roman mosaic and on into Medieval Britain. He had backtracked into the Early Bronze Age (dodging a second guard) and had somehow found his way into Ancient Syria . . . which was indeed seriously ancient. He must have looked at about ten thousand objects all neatly laid out in their glass cases. He felt like a window-shopper in some sort of insane supermarket and he hadn't found anything remotely like Miss Pedicure's statuette. After a while, he barely knew what he was looking at. Whether it was a Late Babylonian jug or an Early Sumerian mug no longer made any difference to him. David had never been very fond of museums. But this was torture.

Standing once again in the entrance hall, he looked at his watch. It was a quarter to eleven. Less than two hours of the challenge remained . . . assuming that Vincent hadn't found the statuette and left with it long ago.

Another guard crossed the entrance hall. "Who's there?" he called out.

David froze. He couldn't be found, not now. But then a second guard, a woman, appeared from the door on the right. "It's only me."

"Wendy? I thought I heard someone . . ."

"Yeah. This place gives me the creeps. I've been hearing things all night. Footsteps . . ."

"Me too. Care for a cup of tea?"

"Yeah. I'll put the kettle on . . ."

The two guards walked off together and David ducked back through another open door just opposite the main entrance. It led into the most amazing room he had ever seen.

It was vast, stretching the entire length of the museum. It was filled with a bizarre collection of animals, people and creatures that were both. Everything looked Egyptian. Huge Pharaohs carved in black stone sat with their hands on their knees, frozen solid as they had been for thousands of years. On one side, two bearded men with lions' feet and dragons' wings crouched, staring at each other in grim silence. On the other, a gigantic tiger stood poised as if about to leap into the darkness. Farther down the gallery there were animals of all shapes and sizes, facing in different directions like guests at a nightmare cocktail party.

David froze. He had seen Vincent before he had heard him. The other boy was moving incredibly quietly and would himself have seen David had he not been looking the other way. David noticed that Vincent had taken his shoes off and was holding them in his hand. It was a good idea and one that David should have thought of himself.

Vincent was looking as lost and as tired as David. Crouching down behind a brass baboon, David watched him pass. As he went, Vincent rubbed his forehead with the back of one hand and David almost felt sorry for him. He had never liked Vincent and he didn't trust him. But he knew what he was going through now.

A minute later Vincent had gone. David stood up. Which way now? Vincent hadn't found the statue yet, and that was good, but it didn't help him. He looked once more at his watch. There was a little over an hour left.

Left or right? Up or down?

At the far end of the gallery he could see a collection of sarcophagi and several obelisks—some carved with hieroglyphics like Cleopatra's Needle—plus four gods with the heads of cats.

And that was when he knew.

In fact he should have known from the start. This challenge was all about skill, not chance. Mr. Helliwell had said it himself: *a test of stealth and cunning*. What he and Mr. Kilgraw had said, what Miss Pedicure had said, and what he had just seen . . . put them all together and the answer was obvious.

David knew where he was going now. He should have known hours ago. He looked around him for a sign, then ran off down the gallery.

He just hoped he wasn't already too late.

Between them, Mr. Kilgraw, Mr. Helliwell and Miss Pedicure had given him all the clues he could have asked for. David played back what they had said.

Some needles are bigger than others . . . that may point you in the right direction.

Well, David had just seen the biggest needle of all—a stone pillar that had made him think of Cleopatra's Needle on the Thames River. And what direction had that come from? Egypt!

And then Miss Pedicure: *It was taken from my mummy . . .*

She wasn't talking about her mother, of course. The

statuette had been buried with her, part of an Egyptian mummy.

That was where he was going now. The head of a giant ram watched him without interest as he plunged into the Egyptian rooms of the museum. The statuette would be somewhere here—he was certain. How could he have wasted so much time? If only he'd stopped and thought first . . .

The first room he entered was filled with more sarcophagi—the stone coffins that contained the mummies. There were about a dozen of them on display, brightly colored and strangely cheerful. It was as if the Ancient Egyptians had chosen to gift wrap their dead. Some of the cases were open, and glancing inside, David saw hunched, shriveled-up figures in dirty gray bandages. Strange to think that Miss Pedicure had once looked like that—although when it was raining and she was in a bad mood, she sometimes still did.

David hurried into the next room. What he was looking for would be displayed separately, in one of the side cases. How much time did he have left? There were still hundreds of objects on display all around him. His eyes raced past dolls, toys, mummified cats and snakes, jugs, cups, jewelry . . . and then he found it! It was right in front of him, a blue figure about the size of his hand, lying on its back as if sunbathing. David rested his hand on the glass and stared at the little doll, at its black hair, thin face and tapered waist. He recognized Miss Pedicure at once. The statue was labeled:

GLAZED COMPANION DOLL. XVIIITH DYNASTY. 1450 B.C.

It was incredible. The English and history teacher had hardly changed in three thousand years. She was even carrying the same handbag.

Somebody coughed at the end of the gallery and David froze. But it was only another guard, making for a side room and an early-twenty-first-century cup of tea. He tilted his watch. It was just after eleven. He had more time than he thought. He lifted the cover of the glass case and took out the statuette.

The Unholy Grail was his.

At half past eleven, David climbed the escalator at the Baker Street subway station and emerged into the street. He had preferred to take the train back to Regent's Park, losing himself in the crowds underground. It was only a ten-minute walk back to the telephone booth. The statuette was safely in his pocket. He had plenty of time.

It was a cool evening with a touch of drizzle in the breeze. David wondered where Vincent might be now. The other boy was probably still in the British Museum, desperately searching for the statue. Even if he did work out the puzzle and find the display case, he was too late. It was too bad. But the best man had won.

A motorcyclist accelerated through a puddle, sending the water in a spray that just missed David. On the other side of the road, a bus without passengers rumbled through a yellow light and turned toward the West End. David continued on past Madame Tussauds. His father had taken him to the famous waxworks museum once, but it hadn't been a successful trip. "Not enough bankers!" Mr. Eliot had exclaimed, and had left without even visiting the Chamber of Horrors. The long, windowless building was silent. The pavement outside, crowded with tourists and ice-cream vendors by day, was empty, glistening under the streetlights.

David felt a gust of cold air tug at the collar of his shirt. Behind him he heard the sound of splintering wood. He thought nothing of it. But unconsciously he quickened his pace.

The road continued up to a set of traffic lights. This was where Regent's Park began—David could see it in the distance, a seemingly endless black space. He glanced behind him. Although the pavement had been empty before, there was now a single figure, staggering about as if drunk. It was a man, wearing some sort of uniform and boots. He was weaving small circles on the pavement, his arms outstretched, his feet jerking into the air. It was as if he had never walked before, as if he were trying to get his balance.

David turned the corner, leaving the drunk—if that was what he was—behind. He was beginning to feel uneasy but he still didn't know why.

The path he was following crossed a main road and then continued over a humpback bridge. Suddenly he was out of the hubbub of London. The darkness and emptiness of Regent's Park was all around him, enclosing him in its ancient arms. Somewhere a dog barked in the night.

"Just slow down . . ."

He muttered the words to himself, somehow relieved to hear the sound of his own voice. Once again he looked at his watch. A quarter to twelve. Plenty of time. How had he allowed one crazy drunk to spook him like this? Smiling, he looked back over his shoulder.

The smile died on his lips.

The man had followed him into the park. He was standing on the bridge now, lit by a lamp directly above him. In the last few minutes he had learned how to walk properly and he was standing at attention, his eyes glittering in the light. He was much closer and David could see him clearly—the brown boots, the belt, the strap running across his chest. He wasn't wearing a uniform but a sort of brown suit, the pants ballooning out at the thighs. David recognized him instantly. He would have known even without the black swastika on the red-and-white armband on the man's right arm. How could he fail to recognize the thin black hair sweeping down over the pale face and, of course, the famous mustache?

Adolf Hitler!

Or at least, Adolf Hitler's waxwork.

David remembered the gust of cold air he had felt. There was always a touch of coldness in the air when black magic was being performed and the blacker the spell the more intense the coldness. He had felt it but he had ignored it. And the splintering sound! The creature must have broken the door to get out. Who could have animated it? Vincent? David stared at the Hitler waxwork, feeling sick. And even as he backed away, a horrible thought occurred to him. Hitler had been first out of Madame Tussauds. But was he alone?

The question was answered a second later. The Hitler waxwork jerked forward, his legs jackknifing in the air. Behind him, two more figures appeared, rising like zombies over the top of the humpback bridge. David didn't wait to see who they might be. Three words were echoing in his mind.

Chamber of Horrors.

He tried to remember who was exhibited in that part of Madame Tussauds. He had a nasty feeling he might be meeting them at any moment.

David turned and ran. But it was only now that he saw how carefully the trap had been laid. Three more waxworks had made their way into the park and were approaching him from the other direction. One was dressed only in a dirty white nightgown and black clogs. It was carrying something in its hands. David stared. It was a victim of the French Revolution. It was carrying its head! Behind it came two short men in prison uniforms. David didn't recognize either of them—but they had recognized him. Their eyes seemed to light up as they shuffled forward, arms outstretched. David saw a gate in the fence, half open. He ran through it and into the inner heart of the park.

He found himself on a patch of lawn with a set of tennis courts to one side and an unpleasant, stagnant pool on the other. The field was dotted with trees and he made for the nearest one, grateful at least that it was a dark night. But even as he ran, the clouds parted and a huge moon broke through like a searchlight. Was that part of the magic too? Was Vincent even controlling the weather?

In the white, ghostly light, the whole park had changed. It was like something out of a bad dream. Everything was black, white and gray. The Hitler waxwork had already reached the gate and passed through with the two prisoners. The French Revolution victim had been left behind. This waxwork had tripped over a tree root and lost its head, and although the head was shouting "Over here!" the rest of the body hadn't found it yet.

But that was the only good news.

Another half-dozen waxworks had somehow found their way to the park and were spreading out, searching through the trees. There was a man dressed entirely in black with a doctor's bag in one hand and a huge, curving knife in the other. Jack the Ripper! And right behind him came a lady in Victorian dress, horribly stabbed, blood (wax blood, David had to remind himself) pouring out of a gaping wound in her chest. She had to be one of the women he had killed. Behind him, David heard a dreadful gurgling sound and turned just in time to see a third, white-faced waxwork rising through the scummy surface of the pool. The models were everywhere. David crouched behind a tree, trying to lose himself in it. He was surrounded and knew that it was only a matter of time before he was found.

"There he is, Adolf!" somebody shouted.

A short, dark-haired man in a double-breasted suit had climbed out of a ditch, an ugly scar twisting down his wax cheek. It was a face that David recognized from old black-and-white films: the American gangster Al Capone. He walked quickly across the grass, then brought his hands up in front of his chest. There was a metallic click. Capone was holding a machine gun. He had just loaded it.

With his breath rasping in his throat, David left the cover of the tree and broke into a run. The wax models were all around him, some like sleepwalkers, others more like clockwork toys as they scuttled forward. He felt horribly exposed out in the moonlight but he had no choice. He had to find the telephone booth, but where was it? He made a quick calculation and started forward, then dived to the ground as a spray of machine-gun bullets sliced through the air, barely an inch above his head. Al Capone had fired at him. And somehow David knew that the bullets were the one thing there that weren't made of wax.

Someone stepped out in front of him, blocking his way. It was a small man in an old-fashioned wing-collar shirt and a stylish gray suit. He had wispy, ginger hair and a small mustache. His eyes twinkled behind round, wire-framed glasses. The man held up the palms of his hands. "It's all right," he said. "I'm a doctor."

"A doctor?" David panted.

"Yes. Dr. Crippen!"

The man had pulled out a vicious-looking hypodermic syringe. David yelled and lashed out with his fist, catching the little man straight on the nose. He felt his fist sink into the soft wax, and when he jerked it back, he had left a round imprint inside the figure's head. David ran. Behind him he could hear Hitler shouting out orders in manic German. Jack the Ripper was lumbering up behind him with the hideous knife raised above his head.

Meanwhile, another man, this one in gleaming silver armor, had just come in through the open gate. He had long black hair, tied behind his neck, and two of the cruelest eyes David had ever seen. Swords and daggers, at least a dozen of them, protruded from him in every direction. It was Attila the Hun, one of the most blood-thirsty warriors in history, and David had no doubt whose blood he was thirsting for now.

The grass curved around behind the tennis courts, bordered on the edge by a thicket of trees and shrubs. David plunged into the shadows, glad to be out of the glare of the moon. The darkness seemed to confuse the waxworks because they hung back, one or two of them bumping into each other, almost as if they were afraid to cross the line from light into dark. There was an iron fence straight ahead of him. David ran over to it, grabbing it with both hands.

His heart was thudding madly in his chest and he stopped to catch his breath and give himself time to think. They hadn't gotten him yet! There was still time to reach the telephone booth and make his way back to Groosham Grange. David jerked one hand down to his pants pocket. The statuette was still there.

Vincent! He breathed the name through clenched teeth. This had to be Vincent's work. He must somehow have followed David from the museum and conjured up the spell as he walked past Madame Tussauds. Of course, he had cheated. Vincent had broken the single rule of the contest—not to use magic—and the worst of it was that there was nothing David could do. What spell could he use to destroy the waxworks? And if he used magic, wouldn't he be disqualifying himself?

David was gripping the fence so hard that the metal bit into his hands. He looked over the top, into the next enclosure, and for the first time since he had reached the park, he felt a surge of hope. The telephone booth was in sight—and it was unguarded. It was only ten to twelve. All he had to do was climb the fence and he would be home free!

He took one last look back. With Hitler at the head of them, just about all the waxworks were congregating on the fence, a semicircle that had already begun to close in. Only two of the waxworks had stayed behind: the drowned man and the Victorian woman. They had found the Frenchman's lost head and, despite his protests, were playing tennis with it on one of the courts. Jack the Ripper was edging forward with a diabolical smile, his wax lips parted to reveal two jagged lines of wax teeth. Dr. Crippen had two more syringes and a surgical knife. Al Capone was behind him, trying to elbow his way past. David wasn't sure if their glass eyes could make him out in the shadows. But slowly they were heading toward him.

It was time to go. He swung around, preparing to heave himself over the fence. Too late. He saw a movement out of the corner of his eye. Something hit him full in the face and he was thrown back, off his feet. For a moment the world spun and then his shoulders hit the earth and all his breath was punched out of him.

"It's all right, everyone! I've got him! Hurry! Come quickly!"

The voice was shrill and excited. There was a rustle of leaves and a snapping of twigs and a large woman dressed in blue stepped forward. David tried to stand but all his strength had left him. The woman was wearing a billowing velvet-and-silk dress that made her look enormous. Her head was crowned by a silver-and-diamond tiara that sparkled even out of the moonlight and there was a Weight Watchers badge pinned to her lapel. She hadn't come out of the Chamber of Horrors. Lying, dazed, on a bed of leaves, David instantly recognized the ginger hair and perfect smile of the Duchess of York. She had hit him with her handbag.

"Good work, Your Highness," Dr. Crippen muttered. His wax nose was bent out of shape where David had hit him and one of his eyes had fallen out.

"*Ja. Sehr gut, Fräulein Fergie,*" Hitler agreed.

David wrenched the statuette out of his pocket and tried to stand up. The park was spinning around him, moving faster and faster. He tried to speak, to utter a few words of some spell that might yet save him. But his mouth was dry and the words would not come. He looked up into the leering, lifeless faces that surrounded him and raised a hand. Then the Duchess hit him again and he was out cold.

He's lying," David said. "I found the statuette. He stole it. And he used magic to do it."

David was standing in Mr. Kilgraw's study with Vincent only a few paces away. His clothes were disheveled and there was a large bruise above his cheek where the handbag had hit him. Mr. Helliwell stood in one corner of the room, resting his chin on one hand, watching the two boys quietly. Mr. Kilgraw sat behind his desk with the statuette in front of him. David felt like snapping it in half. And he felt much the same about Vincent.

"I admit he found it first," Vincent said. He took his hands out of his pockets. "I've told you. I worked out the puzzle and found the cabinet, but I was too late. I guessed

David had taken it, so I went back to the telephone booth. That was when I saw him with the statuette lying next to him. I figure he must have tripped over or something, so I took the statuette. I didn't see any waxworks, though," he added.

"Didn't see them?" David curled his fists. "You sent them!"

"I had nothing to do with it."

"Then who did?"

"That's enough of this!" Mr. Kilgraw said, fluttering his hand for silence. His voice was little more than a whisper, but then the assistant headmaster rarely spoke loudly. He leaned back in his chair. "The trial is over," he said. "And Vincent has won."

"But, sir . . ." David began.

"No!" Mr. Kilgraw pointed a finger. "David, you talk about cheating, but it seems to me that it was only a few days ago that you were discovered trying to steal the papers for the last exam."

"That was Vincent too," David replied. "He set me up."

"And then there's the question of Sports Day. The obstacle course . . ."

David fell silent. He was blushing and he knew it.

The obstacle course! Mr. Kilgraw had known about it all the time. There was nothing David could say now. He had cheated once in his life, and because of that, nobody would ever trust him again.

"We don't need to prolong this discussion," Mr. Kilgraw said. "Whatever happened tonight, Vincent won. He was the first back and he brought the statue with him. Mr. Helliwell . . . ?"

In the corner, the voodoo teacher shrugged. "I'm sorry, David," he said. "But I have to agree."

"Then that's that. Vincent King takes first place in the standings. At prize-giving it will be he who is presented with the Unholy Grail."

"Thank you, sir." Vincent glanced again at David. "I mean it, David," he said. "I didn't want it to happen this way."

"Like hell . . ."

"Don't ever compare anything to hell until you've been there!" Mr. Kilgraw snapped, and now he was really angry. "I have to say you've been a complete disappointment, David. And not just tonight. Fighting in the corridor. Trying to steal the exam questions and then whining and complaining when you failed to answer all the questions. You used to be our most promising pupil.

But now I even wonder if it's worth your staying here at Groosham Grange."

"So do I," David growled. He regretted the words as soon as they were out, but it was too late. Mr. Kilgraw had heard.

"That's a decision you have to make," he said. "If you want to leave, nobody will stop you. But remember, once you've gone, you can't come back. We'll never see you again . . ."

David opened his mouth to speak, but there was nothing to say. He took one last look at Vincent, who was doing his best to avoid his eyes. Mr. Helliwell sighed and shook his head. Mr. Kilgraw's hand closed round the statuette. "And now if you'll excuse me," he said, "this has to go back to the museum. It'll be daylight soon and we wouldn't want it to be missed."

Jill Green was waiting for David outside the study. She was about to ask him what had happened, but one look at his face told her all she needed to know.

"So he won, then," she said.

David nodded.

"Does it really matter, David? I mean, what's so important about the Unholy Grail anyway?" She took his arm. "You're still the best magician in the school. You don't need a cup to prove it."

"I told Mr. Kilgraw I wanted to leave Groosham Grange," David said.

"What?" Jill stiffened beside him, genuinely shocked.

David sighed. "I didn't know what I was saying, but . . . you remember when we first came here? We didn't want to be witches or magicians. We hated it here!"

"That was before we knew about our powers."

"Yes. And now we're happy here. But that means we've changed, Jill. Maybe we've changed for the worse. Maybe we've become . . ."

"What?"

"It doesn't matter."

But lying in bed, two hours later, David couldn't get the thought out of his mind. Had he become evil? It was true that he had cheated in the race, and despite what Jill had said, he would have done anything to get his hands on the Unholy Grail. Even the name worried him. Unholy. Did it also describe him?

What is good and what is evil? Sometimes it's not as easy as you think to tell them apart . . .

He remembered what Mr. Fitch (or was it Mr. Teagle?)

had said to him, but he still wasn't sure what the head had meant. Good or evil? Stay or go? Why did everything have to be so complicated?

On the other side of the dormitory, Vincent turned in his sleep and pulled the sheets over him. David thought back to their first meeting. Vincent had arrived one July morning, carried over on the ferry that connected Skrull Island with the mainland. Handsome, athletic and quiet, Vincent seemed to fit in much faster than David had. In just a few weeks he had found his way through the mirror in the library and been given his own black ring. Maybe that was part of the trouble. The two of them had been in competition almost from the start and David had never bothered to find out anything about him—his home life, his parents, where he had come from.

How had he come to mistrust Vincent? Because of the East Tower. He had spotted Vincent coming out of the forbidden tower, next to the school's graveyard, and that had been the start of it. There was some sort of mystery connected with the place. Gregor knew. The school porter had stopped David from going in.

David pushed his covers back and got out of bed. It was three o'clock in the morning; a cold, foggy night. He was probably crazy. But he couldn't sleep anyway and he had nothing else to do. Whatever Vincent was really up to, he would find the answer in the East Tower. And he would go there now.

The night was bitterly cold. As David tiptoed through the school's graveyard his breath frosted and hung in the air around his head. Somewhere an owl hooted. A fat spider clambered down one of the gravestones and disappeared into the soil. Something moved at the edge of the graveyard. David froze. But it was only a ghost, leaving its grave for a few hours' haunting. It hadn't seen him. Slowly, he moved on.

And there was the East Tower, looming out of the darkness ahead of him. David gazed at the crooked brickwork, the tangle of dark green ivy that surrounded it, the empty windows and, far above him, the broken battlements. He checked one last time. There was nobody around. He moved toward the entrance.

The only way into the East Tower was through a curved oak door, at least three feet thick. David was sure it would be locked, but no sooner had he touched it than it swung inward, its iron hinges creaking horribly.

There was something very creepy about the sound. For a moment he was tempted to go back to bed. But it was too late now. He had to settle this. He stepped inside.

The inner chamber of the tower was pitch-black. A few tiny shafts of moonlight penetrated the cracks in the brickwork, but the central area was a gaping hole. David didn't have a flashlight or even a box of matches with him. But he didn't need them. He closed his eyes and whispered a few words set down by the Elizabethan magician called John Dee. When he opened them again, the interior glowed with a strange green light. It was still gloomy but he could see.

The lower floor was empty, the ground strewn with rubble, a few nettles and poisonous herbs poking through. David sniffed the air. Although it was faint, there was something that he recognized, a smell that was at once familiar and yet strange. There was a sound somewhere high above, a sort of fluttering and a high-pitched whine. Ahead of him, a stone staircase climbed upward, spiraling around on itself. David knew that the whole building was condemned, that any one of the stone slabs could crumble and send him crashing to certain death. But there was no other way. He had no choice.

He began to climb the stairs. The East Tower was six

hundred feet high. The staircase, pinned precariously to the outer wall, seemed to go on forever and David was beginning to get dizzy when at last he found himself at the top. There was a coin in his pants pocket and on an impulse he flicked it over his shoulder, into the hole at the center of the stairs.

"One . . . two . . . three . . . four . . . five . . ."

It was a long time before the coin reached the bottom and tinkled on the concrete floor below.

Something moved. David heard a thin clatter like two pieces of cardboard being ruffled against each other. One step at a time, he moved across the concrete flagstones of the upper chamber. He had forgotten to put on any socks and he could feel the frozen air writhing around his ankles. For a second time he heard the strange, high-pitched whining. It was some sort of animal. What animal? What was this place?

He was in a completely circular room. Two of the narrow windows, quite close to each other, had moldered, and now there was only a large, irregular gap. Opposite this, right up against the wall, there was a long wooden table with what looked like two or three baskets on top. Also on the table were an open book, a pile of paper, two candles, a quill pen and a leather-bound book.

David whispered three words. The candles ignited.

It was easier after that. David crossed over to the table and picked up one of the baskets. He felt something flutter between his hands. The front of the basket was a barred door, closed with a twist of wire. David looked inside and now saw what the animal was. A bat. Blind and frightened, it tried to fly, ricocheting off the sides of the cage.

What was Vincent doing with a collection of bats? David put down the cage and went over to the book. He scooped it up and examined it. It was an old exercise book, each page packed with writing so cramped and tiny that it was unreadable. David flicked through the pages. At last he arrived at a section he could read in the light of the candles. A poem:

Beware the shadow that is found
Stretching out across the ground
Where Saint Augustine once began
And four knights slew a holy man
For if the Grail is carried here
Then Groosham Grange will disappear

The Grail! Groosham Grange . . . What did it all mean?

David concentrated on the text. Saint Augustine. He was the man who had brought Christianity to England in the first century. But where had he begun? David racked his brain, trying to remember his history lessons with Miss Pedicure. Augustine had first landed in Thanet, Kent. But that wasn't right. Of course . . . it was Canterbury! Canterbury Cathedral where four knights had slain Thomas à Becket during the reign of Henry II. Suddenly it was all crystal clear.

Carry the Unholy Grail into the shadow of Canterbury Cathedral and the school would disappear!

So that was what Vincent was planning. He wanted to destroy the school and had learned that the only way to do it was to get his hands on the Grail. But first he had to get rid of David—and he had done that brilliantly, baiting him to start with, then framing him and finally cheating him. In just three days' time, Vincent would be presented with his prize. And what then? Somehow he would smuggle it off the island. He would carry it to Canterbury. And then . . .

But what about the bats?

David put down the book and went over to the pile of paper. Paper, candles and bats. They were right next to one another. And when you added them together, what did you get? Candles to see by. Paper to write on. Bats to . . .

"Homing bats," he muttered. Why not? Homing bats were more reliable than homing pigeons. And they were perfect for carrying secret messages. They preferred the dark.

David felt in his pants pocket and pulled out a pencil. It was such an old trick that he was almost ashamed to be trying it. Softly, he scribbled the pencil along the top sheet on the pile of paper, shading it gray. When he had penciled over the entire sheet, he picked it up and held it against the candle flame.

It had worked. David could read five faint lines written in the same tight hand as the notebook:

EVEN MORE TOP SECRET
THAN USUAL
To the Bishop of Bletchley
David Eliot is out of the running. The Grail will be delivered on prize-giving day. Departure from the island will proceed as planned. Am confident that a few days from now, Groosham Grange will no longer exist.

The note was signed with a cross.

Smiling to himself, David wandered over to the broken window and gazed out into the night. Just a few hours before, he had been considering packing his bags and leaving the school. Everything was different now. The sheet of paper and the notebook were all he needed. Once he showed them to the heads, the truth would come out.

What happened next took him completely by surprise. One moment he was standing on the edge of the tower. The next he was toppling forward as something—someone—crashed into the small of his back. He hadn't seen them. He hadn't heard them. For a second or two his hands flailed at the empty air. He tried to regain his balance, but then whoever it was pushed him again and he fell out of the window, away from the tower, into the night.

He was dead. A fall of six hundred feet onto the cold earth below would kill him for sure. The wind rushed into his face and the whole world twisted upside down. There was no time to utter a spell, no time to do anything.

With a last, despairing cry, he thrust his hand out, grabbing at the darkness, not expecting to find anything. But there was something. His fingers closed. Somehow his arm had caught a branch of ivy. He gripped tighter. He was still falling, pulling the ivy away with him as he went. But the farther he fell, the thicker the ivy became. He was tangled up in it and it was slowing him down. More branches wrapped themselves around his chest and his waist. He came to a halt. With the ground only a hundred feet away, the ivy reclaimed him, springing him back, crashing him into the brickwork. David shouted with pain. His arm had almost been torn out of its socket. But a few moments later he found himself dangling in midair. He was no longer falling. He was alive.

It took him thirty minutes to disentangle himself and climb the rest of the way down, and when he finally found himself on the ground once again, he felt dizzy and sick. He took a deep breath, then looked back up. The window where he had been pushed was almost out of sight, terribly high up. It was a miracle that he was alive at all.

Even so, he knew what he had to do. As much as the idea appalled him, he had to be certain and so, forcing himself on, he went back into the East Tower and all the way back up the stairs. The top chamber was empty this time. And his worst fears had been realized. The pile of papers, the bats and the notebook were gone.

The orange Rolls-Royce was tearing up the highway at a hundred miles an hour. All around it, cars were hooting, swerving and crashing into the hard shoulder as they tried to get out of the way.

"Shouldn't you be driving on the *left* side of the road, dear?" Mrs. Eliot demanded.

"Nonsense," Mr. Eliot replied, poking her with the cigarette lighter. "We're part of Europe now. I drive on the right in France and Switzerland. I don't see why I shouldn't do the same here."

Mrs. Eliot's false eyelashes fluttered as a tractor trailer jackknifed out of their path, its horn blaring. "I think I'm going to be sick," she muttered.

"Well, put your head out of the window," Mr. Eliot snapped. "And this time remember to open the window first."

Edward and Eileen Eliot were on their way to Norfolk in their specially converted Rolls-Royce. Mr. Eliot was unable to walk, which would have been sad except that he had never really liked walking in the first place and much preferred his wheelchair. He was a short, round man with more hair in his nostrils than on his head. His wife, Eileen, was much taller than him with so many false parts—hair, teeth, nails, eyelashes—that it was hard to be sure what she looked like at all.

They were not alone in the car. Wedged into the very corner of the backseat was a small, shriveled woman in a drab cotton dress. She had pale cheeks, crooked teeth and hair that could have fallen off a horse. This was Mildred Eliot, Edward's sister. After eleven years of marriage, her husband had recently died of boredom. Mildred had talked all the way through the funeral and had only stopped when one of the undertakers had finally hit her with a spade.

"What's that funny rattling noise, Edward?" she asked now as the car turned off the highway, went the wrong way around a roundabout and raced through a set of red lights.

"What rattling noise?" Mr. Eliot demanded.

"I think it must be the engine," Mildred sniffed. "Personally I don't trust these English cars," she went on in her thin, whiny voice. "They're so unreliable. Why didn't you buy a nice Japanese car, Edward? The Japanese know how to build cars. Why didn't you—"

"Unreliable!" Mr. Eliot screamed, interrupting her. He wrenched the steering wheel, sending the car off the road and onto the sidewalk. "This is a Rolls-Royce you're talking about! Do you know how much a Rolls-Royce costs? It costs thousands! I didn't eat for a month after I bought my Rolls-Royce. I couldn't afford gas for three years!"

"They're very reliable," Eileen Eliot agreed, sticking her finger into the cigarette lighter to demonstrate. There was a flash as the dashboard short-circuited and she electrocuted herself.

"The Japanese couldn't build a Rolls-Royce in a thousand years," Mr. Eliot continued, unplugging his wife. "In fact they couldn't even pronounce it!" He jammed his foot down on the accelerator, but he must have taken a wrong turn as he was now shooting through a playground with mothers and children hurling themselves into the flower beds to get out of the way. "What sort of road is this?" he demanded angrily.

"The Japanese have marvelous roads," Mildred remarked. "And bullet trains . . ."

"I'll bullet you . . ." Mr. Eliot growled. He stamped down and the Rolls-Royce smashed through a fence, leaped over the sidewalk and headed on toward the Norfolk coast.

Two hours later, they arrived.

Because it was on an island, Groosham Grange was unreachable by car—even by Rolls-Royce—and the last part of the journey had to be undertaken by boat. Mr. Eliot had parked right beside the sea and now he wheeled himself down to a twisting wooden jetty that jutted out precariously over the water. There was a boat waiting for them—an old fisherman's trawler. The old fisherman was sitting inside.

Seeing Mr. Eliot, he stood up. "More parents?" he demanded.

Mr. Eliot examined the man with distaste. He looked like something out of a pirate film, what with his black beard and single gold earring. "Yes," he said. "Will you ferry us over?"

"I will. I'll ferry you there. I'll ferry you back. I been doing it all day." The man spat. "Parents! Who needs 'em!"

"What's your name?" Mr. Eliot demanded.

"Bloodbath. Captain Bloodbath." The captain squinted. "And I take it that's your lovely wife?"

Mr. Eliot glanced at Mildred, who was standing beside him. She had a large, bulging handbag on her arm. "She's not my wife and she's not lovely," he replied. "My wife is under the car."

"I've fixed it!" Eileen Eliot called out and sat up, banging her head on the exhaust with a dull clang. There was oil on her dress and more on her face. She had a wrench in one hand and another one between her teeth. "I think you must have cracked a cylinder when you ran over that cyclist," she said, joining the others on the jetty.

"Typical English workmanship," Mildred muttered.

Mr. Eliot took one of the wrenches and hit her with it. "Let's get on the boat," he said.

A few minutes later, Captain Bloodbath cast off, and

belching black smoke and rumbling, the boat began the crossing. The captain sat at the front, steering, and Mr. Eliot was surprised to see that his hands seemed to be made of steel.

"They're ally-minium!" Bloodbath exclaimed, noticing the banker staring at him. He clapped his hands together with a loud ping. "My own hands was pulled off a year ago. Lost at sea. The boys made these ones for me in metalwork class. Very handy they are too!"

"Delightful," Mrs. Eliot agreed with a weak smile.

There was a slight mist on the water, but as they chugged forward, it suddenly parted. And there were the soaring cliffs of Skrull Island with the waves crashing and frothing on the jagged black rocks below. The boat pulled into a second jetty and then there was a five-minute drive up the steep road to the school with Gregor, who was simpering and sniggering at the wheel.

"I'm not sure I think too much of the staff," Mrs. Eliot whispered. "I mean, that man with no hands! And unless I'm mistaken, this driver is completely deformed!"

The car stopped. Mildred uttered a little scream and leaped out.

"What's happened?" Mr. Eliot exclaimed. "Has she been stung by a wasp?"

"It's David!" Mildred threw her hands up above her head. "Oh, David! I hardly recognized you!" she warbled. She slapped her hands limply against her cheeks. "You've grown so tall! And you've put on weight! And your hair's so long. You've completely changed!"

"That's because I'm not David," the boy she was talking to said. "That's David over there . . ."

"Oh . . ."

By this time, Mr. Eliot had been helped out of the car and he and Eileen Eliot were looking uncertainly at the school. The sun was shining and the whole building had been decked out for the day with a few strips of bunting and flags. A refreshment tent had been set up in the grounds. But even so it still looked rather grim.

David walked over to them. "Hello, Mother," he said. "Hello, Father. Hello, Aunt Mildred."

Mr. Eliot eyed his son critically. "How many prizes have you won?" he asked.

David sighed. "I'm afraid I haven't won any."

"Not any!" Mr. Eliot exploded. "That's it, then! Back in the car! We're going home."

"But we only just got here," his wife protested.

Mr. Eliot wheeled over her foot. "Well, we're off again," he yelled. "I won a prize every year I was at

133

Beton College. I won prizes for history, geometry and French. I even won prizes for winning prizes! If I hadn't won a prize, my father would have sliced me open with a surgical knife and confiscated one of my kidneys!"

By now Mr. Eliot had gone bright red. He seemed to be having difficulty breathing and his whole face was contorted with pain. Mrs. Eliot took out a bottle of pills and forced several of them into his mouth. "You shouldn't upset your father, David," she said. "You know he has trouble with his blood pressure. Sometimes his blood doesn't have any pressure at all!"

"I'm sorry," David muttered.

By the time Mr. Eliot had recovered, Gregor had taken the car back to the jetty to fetch another batch of parents and so he was forced to stay. Fortunately for David, Mr. Helliwell chose that moment to come over and introduce himself. The voodoo teacher was dressed in his fanciest clothes for prize-giving: black suit and tails, wing collar and, perched on his head, a crooked black hat. He had also painted his face white with black rings around his eyes. Both Mildred and Mrs. Eliot trembled as he approached, but Mr. Helliwell couldn't have been more friendly. "You should be very proud of David," he said.

"Why?" Mr. Eliot asked.

"He's coming along very well." Mr. Helliwell smiled, showing a line of teeth like tombstones. "He may have been unlucky, not getting the prize, but otherwise he's had a good year. I'm sure he'll get a good report card."

David was grateful to the teacher despite himself. But he still couldn't meet Mr. Helliwell's eyes. The memory of the trial and what had happened afterward was still too raw.

"Perhaps you would like me to show you around the school," Mr. Helliwell said.

"Around it?" Mrs. Eliot asked. "Why can't we go in it?"

"He means in it, you idiotic woman," Mr. Eliot snapped.

"This way . . ." Mr. Helliwell winked at David, then began to push the wheelchair. Eileen Eliot and Mildred followed.

"They have much more modern schools in Tokyo," Mildred said. She pulled her handbag farther up her arm. "The Japanese have a wonderful education system . . ."

And then they were gone, entering the building

through one of the open doors. They had quite forgotten David. But that suited him fine. The day was moving too fast. He needed time to think.

There were about thirty-five sets of parents on the island, more than eighty people in all, what with various aunts, uncles and friends. All of them were milling about in their best clothes, the women with hats and handbags, the men smug and smiling. Of course, they weren't going to be allowed to see everything. A lot of the school's equipment—the skulls, five-fingered candleholders, wands, magic circles and the rest of it—had been hidden away. For the next ten minutes they would wander around the grounds and then they would all assemble in the large tent where Mr. Kilgraw would make a speech and Vincent King would be awarded the Unholy Grail.

David knew that this would be the critical moment. It would be the only time when Vincent would have the Grail in his hands. If he was going to get it off the island, he would have to do it today.

And that was the one thing he still didn't know. How did Vincent plan to remove the Grail?

It seemed to him that there was only one way—in Captain Bloodbath's boat. But that had been kept well secured ever since David himself had stolen it a while back. So what was Vincent going to do? David had been surprised to discover that Vincent's parents weren't coming to prize-giving—so they couldn't take it for him. But perhaps he had someone in the crowd: a fake uncle or aunt. Perhaps the Bishop of Bletchley himself was here, in disguise. Even now he could be waiting to seize it. And with so many people coming and going, it would be easy to smuggle it away.

But David had no idea what the Bishop looked like— in disguise or out of it. There were plenty of parents with white hair and saintly faces. He could be any one of them. David glanced at the tent. Vincent was standing in the sunlight with Monsieur Leloup, looking very dashing in a blazer and white pants. The French teacher was introducing him to a group of parents, obviously flattering him. David felt a surge of jealousy. That should have been him.

"Seen anything?"

Jill had come up behind him and caught hold of his arm. David had told her everything that had happened the morning after his fall from the East Tower. Only Jill, his closest friend on the island, would have believed him—and even she had taken a lot of persuading. But in the end she had agreed to help.

David shook his head. "No. Everything's so ordinary. But I know it's going to happen, Jill. And soon . . ."

"Maybe you should go to the heads, David."

"And tell them what?" David sighed. "They'd never listen to me."

"Look out!" Jill gestured in the direction of the school. "I think your parents are coming back."

"Do you want to meet them?"

"No thanks." Jill hurried off. She stopped a few paces away and turned round. "Don't worry, David," she said. "I'll keep an eye on Vincent."

Over by the tent, Vincent glanced suddenly toward them. Had he overheard what she had just said?

But then Mr. Helliwell reached David, still pushing his father in the wheelchair.

"An excellent school," Mr. Eliot was saying. "I am most impressed. Of course, it is a little unnatural for boys and girls to be here together. At Beton College, where I went, there were only boys. In fact, even the headmaster's wife was a boy. But I suppose that's progress . . ."

"Absolutely." Mr. Helliwell smiled politely. "Now, if you'll excuse me . . ." The teacher hurried off toward the tent.

Mr. Eliot turned to his son. "Well, David," he said. "I can see it was a good decision to send you here."

"Your father does make wonderful decisions," Mrs. Eliot agreed.

"I have suggested to Mr. Helliwell a little more use of the cane," Mr. Eliot went on. He nodded to himself. "What I always say is that a good beating never hurt anyone."

Mrs. Eliot frowned. "But, darling, if it didn't hurt, how could it be a good beating?"

"No, my love. What I mean is—"

But before Mr. Eliot could either explain or demonstrate what he meant, a bell rang. The prize-giving was about to begin.

Mr. and Mrs. Eliot, Mildred and David joined the other parents. What with the narrow entrance and the number of people trying to get in, it was another quarter of an hour before they finally took their places. David looked around him, at the rows of seats stretched out underneath the canvas and the platform raised at the far end with the staff of Groosham Grange taking their places along it. He saw Vincent, sitting on his own. Then Mr. Kilgraw stood up and everyone hushed.

But already there was something wrong. David looked

one way, then another. Something had caught his eye. What was it? And then he saw, right at the back, near the entrance, an empty seat.

Mr. Kilgraw had begun to speak, but David didn't hear a word. He was scanning the audience, searching through the faces, the boys and the girls, the teachers and the parents . . .

But she wasn't there. The empty seat.

Jill had promised to keep an eye on Vincent. Vincent had overheard her. And now Jill had disappeared.

Canterbury
Cathedral

Sports Day

Flying Lesson

Vincent

Departure

Wax

Cracks

Needle in
a Haystack

Pursuit

The Exam

On the Rocks

The East
Tower

Prize-Giving

Good afternoon, ladies and gentlemen," Mr. Kilgraw began. The flaps had been drawn across the tent to protect him from the sun, but just to be safe he was also wearing a slightly incongruous straw hat. "Welcome to Groosham Grange on this, our annual prize-giving day. May I begin by apologizing on behalf of the heads, Mr. Fitch and Mr. Teagle, who are unable to attend today. Mr. Fitch has yellow fever. Mr. Teagle has scarlet fever. If they get too close to each other, they go a nasty shade of orange.

"This has been a very successful year for Groosham Grange. Some might even say a magical year. I am pleased to tell you that our new biology laboratory has been built by workmen who were actually created in our old biology laboratory. Well done, eleventh graders! Our Ecology Club has been busy and we now have our own Tropical Rain Forest on the south side of the island. Congratulations also to the Drama Club. They really brought *Frankenstein* to life. So, for that matter, did our physics class.

"It's not all work at Groosham Grange, of course. Our French class visited France. Our Ancient Greek class visited Ancient Greece. A school inspector visited us. And if you happen to pass through the cemetery, I hope you'll visit him. As usual, our staff has made many sacrifices. I would like to thank them and I ought also to thank the sacrifices . . ."

David found it hard to concentrate on what Mr. Kilgraw was saying. He was sitting between his mother and father. Aunt Mildred, who was next to Edward Eliot, had already fallen asleep and was whistling softly through her nose. David was in the middle of the tent, completely surrounded by parents: bald parents, fat parents, parents with red veins in their noses and wax in their ears, parents in expensive jewelry and expensive suits. He felt as if he was drowning in parents. Was this what he would be like one day? It was a horrible thought.

And it didn't make it any easier to think. David knew that the next few minutes would be critical. Once Vincent had the Unholy Grail, anything could happen. How would Vincent get the Grail off the island? Would he carry it himself, slipping away with the crowd? Or would he pass it to someone in the crowd—and if so, who? And what about Jill? David wanted to get up and look for her now, but he knew that he couldn't. He was too close to Vincent. He was trapped.

"At Groosham Grange there is only one winner," Mr. Kilgraw was saying. "And there is only one prize . . ."

David turned his attention back to the platform and saw that the assistant headmaster was holding something in his hands. Even from this distance he knew what it was. For the parents—bored and beginning to fidget—it was no more than a silver chalice decorated with red stones. But for David, the Unholy Grail seemed to glow with a light of its own. He could feel it reaching out to him. He had never wanted anything so much in his entire life.

"It is the school's most valued trophy," Mr. Kilgraw went on. "In fact you could say that without it there would be no Groosham Grange. Every year it is presented to the student whose work, whose general behavior and whose overall contribution to school life has put him or her at the top of the class. This year, the contest was particularly close . . ."

Was David imagining it or did Mr. Kilgraw search him out, his eyes glittering as they locked into David's? It was almost a challenge. For the space of a heartbeat the two of them were alone beneath the canvas. The parents had gone. Vincent had gone. And David's hands twitched, reaching out to take what was rightfully his.

Then it was over.

". . . but it gives me great pleasure to announce that the winner, our most distinguished pupil is—Vincent King!"

David reluctantly joined in the general applause, at the same time trying to smile. Vincent stood up and went onto the stage. He shook hands with Mr. Kilgraw. Mr. Kilgraw muttered a few words. Vincent took the Grail and sat down again. The applause died away. And that was it. The Unholy Grail was his.

Mr. Kilgraw spoke for another five minutes and David counted every one of them. The prize-giving might be over, but he knew that his work was only beginning. Whatever happened, he intended to stick close to

Vincent—and to the Grail. He would just have to worry about Jill later.

But it wasn't as easy as David had hoped. As soon as Mr. Kilgraw had finished his speech, everyone stood up at once in a rush for the sherry and sausage rolls that Gregor and Mrs. Windergast were serving at the back of the tent. At the same time, Vincent was surrounded by people, examining the Grail and congratulating him, and it was as much as David could do to keep sight of him at all.

Worse than that, he still had his parents to deal with. Mr. Eliot was in a bad mood. "I am disappointed," he was saying as he tore a sausage roll into shreds. "I wish I wasn't your father, to be frank. In fact I wish I was Frank's father. He won three prizes at Beton College."

"I just hope the neighbors don't find out," Mrs. Eliot wept, gnawing at her fingers. "My own son! I can't bear it! We'll have to move. I'll change my name. I'll have plastic surgery . . ."

Aunt Mildred nodded in agreement. "My neighbor's children won *lots* of prizes," she announced. "But then, of course, they have a Japanese au pair . . ."

David craned his neck, searching for a gap between

the three of them. The crowd that had formed around Vincent had separated again and suddenly Vincent had gone. David wasn't sure how he'd done it. But he had left the tent.

Then Gregor limped over to them with a tray of food. "Sumfink tweet?" he gurgled.

"What?" Aunt Mildred asked.

"He's asking if you want something to eat," David translated. He glanced at the tray. "It's toad-in-the-hole," he said. "And I think Gregor's used real toads."

"I think it's time we went," Mildred whispered, going rather green.

Ten minutes later, David saw his parents into the car that would take them back down to the jetty and the boat.

"Good-bye, David," his father said. "I'm afraid I have not enjoyed seeing you. I can see now that your mother and I have always spoiled you."

"We ruined you," Mrs. Eliot wept. Her makeup was flowing in rivers down her cheeks.

"I blame myself," Mr. Eliot went on. "I should have beaten you more. My father beat me every day of my life. He used to buy cane furniture so that he could beat me with the chairs when he wasn't sitting on them. He knew a thing or two about discipline. *Whack! Whack! Whack!* That's all boys understand. Start at the bottom, that's what I say . . ."

"Don't excite yourself, dear," Mrs. Eliot murmured.

Just then Aunt Mildred came running up to the car. "Sorry I'm late," she whined in her thin, nasal voice. "I couldn't find my handbag. Bye bye, dear." She pecked David on the cheek. "Do come and visit me in Margate soon." She got into the car, heaving her handbag onto her lap. "I'm sure it wasn't as heavy as this when I set out this morning," she prattled on. "I can't think how I lost it. That nice teacher found it for me. Honestly, I'd forget my own head if it wasn't . . ."

She was still talking when Gregor started the car and they rattled off down the hill. David watched them until they were out of sight. Then he set off in the direction of the school.

Where could Vincent have gone?

David's first thought was the jetty, but he decided not to go down there yet. He didn't want to follow his parents and the more he thought about it the less likely it was that Vincent would try to stow away on the boat. Captain Bloodbath was too careful—and anyway, it would be far easier to give the Grail to someone else and let them carry it for him. Vincent had to be somewhere in the school. David would find him and confront him with what he knew. But he had to move fast.

First he checked the tent. The parents were starting to thin out, a few clusters of them still chatting with the staff, the rest walking with their sons and daughters toward the jetty. Mr. Kilgraw had left. He would have gone inside to escape the sunlight. Mrs. Windergast was still there, clearing away the food, and David went over to her.

"Excuse me," he said. "Have you seen Vincent?"

The matron smiled at him. "Not for a while, my dear. I suppose you want to congratulate him."

"Not exactly." David left the tent.

In the next half hour he tried the library, the dormitory, the dining room, the hallways and the classrooms. He looked into the heads' study and Mr. Kilgraw's study. Both rooms were empty. Then he tried the cemetery at the edge of the wood. There was no sign of Vincent.

David walked back to the school, feeling increasingly uncomfortable. Everything felt wrong. It was about two o'clock and the sun was shining, but there was no warmth in the air, and no breeze, not even the faintest whisper of one. The light hitting the school was hard, unsparing. It was as if he had stepped out of real life and into a photograph, as if he were the only living thing.

He heard a sound high up, a faint rattling. He looked up, then blinked as something hit him on the side of the cheek. He rubbed the skin with the tips of his fingers. He had been hit by a pebble and a scattering of dust, but he was unhurt. He squinted up in the direction of the sound. One wall of Groosham Grange loomed high above him, a gray gargoyle jutting out at the corner. There was a crack in the brickwork. It was only a small crack, zigzagging horizontally under the gargoyle, but David was sure it hadn't been there before. It looked too fresh, the edges pink against the gray surface of the bricks. It was no more than four inches long. It was a crack, that was all.

But even as David lowered his head there was another soft rattle and a second shower of dust. He looked up again and saw that the crack had lengthened, curving up around the gargoyle. At the same time a second crack had formed a few inches below. Even as he watched, a few pieces of mortar detached themselves from the wall and tumbled down to the earth below. And now there were three cracks, the longest about six feet and perhaps a half inch wide. The gargoyle was surrounded by them.

Its bulging eyes and twisted mouth almost looked afraid.

Suddenly David knew. He remembered the verse:

For if the Grail is carried here
Then Groosham Grange will disappear

The disappearance of Groosham Grange had begun.
The Unholy Grail had already left the island.

The question was, had Vincent gone with it? David knew that he had to find the other boy fast. How far away was Canterbury? He had no doubt that the Grail was already on its way there. Perhaps it was already too late.

But with the onrush of panic came another thought. He had forgotten to look in the one place where he was most likely to find Vincent, the one place that had been tied in with the mystery from the start: the East Tower. Even if the Grail had gone, Vincent might be hiding out there, and if he could just find Vincent, he might yet be able to recapture the Grail. David broke into a run. As he went, a fourth, larger crack opened up in the wall just beside his head.

He reached the door of the tower and without stopping to think, kicked it open and ran in. After the brightness of the afternoon light, the darkness inside the building was total. For about five seconds David was completely blind and in that time he realized three things.

First, that Vincent had been there recently. There was a smell in the air, the same smell that David had noticed the night he had nearly been killed.

Second, that he should have gone in more cautiously and allowed his eyes time to get used to the darkness.

And third, that he was not alone.

The hand that reached out and grabbed him by the throat was invisible. Before he could utter a sound, a second hand clamped itself over his mouth. This hand was holding a pad of material soaked in something that smelled of rotting fruit and alcohol. And as David choked and struggled and slipped into unconsciousness, he thought to himself that the hand was very big, surely far too big to belong to Vincent.

But if it wasn't Vincent, who on earth could it be?

Framed

Canterbury
Cathedral

Sports Day

Flying Lesson

Vincent

Departure

Wax

Needle in
a Haystack

Graves

Pursuit

The Exam

On the Rocks

The East
Tower

Prize-Giving

David's arms, wrists and shoulders were hurting. It was the pain that woke him—that and someone calling his name. He opened his eyes and found himself hunched up on the floor with his back against the wall of a room that he recognized. He was in the upper chamber of the East Tower. Somebody had knocked him out, carried him upstairs, tied him up and left him there.

But who?

All along he had been certain that Vincent King was his secret enemy and that it had been Vincent who was plotting to steal the Grail. Now, at last, he knew that he had been wrong. For there was Vincent right opposite him, also tied up, his hair for once in disarray and an ugly bruise on the side of his face. Jill was sitting next to him, in a similar state. She was the one calling to him.

David straightened himself. "It's all right," he said. "I'm awake."

He tried to separate his wrists but it was impossible. They were tied securely behind his back with some sort of rough rope. He could feel it cutting into his flesh and it was as much as he could do to wiggle his fingers. He pushed himself farther up against the wall, using the heel of his shoe against the rough flagstones. "Just give me a few seconds," he said. He shut his eyes again and whispered the first few words of a spell that would bring a minor Persian demon to his assistance.

"Forget it," Vincent cut in, and David stopped in surprise. The other boy had hardly ever talked to him. Usually they did their best to avoid each other. But now it seemed that they were on the same side. Even so, Vincent sounded tired and defeated. "If you're trying some magic, it won't work," he said. "I've already tried."

"Look at the door," Jill said.

David twisted his head around uncomfortably. There was a shape painted on the closed door. It looked like an eye with a wavy line through it.

"It's the eye of Horus," Vincent said. "It creates a magical barrier. It means—"

"—it means we can't use our powers," David concluded. He nodded. "I know."

Gritting his teeth, he seesawed his wrists together, trying to loosen the rope. It cost him a few inches of skin and gave him little in return. His hands had rotated and his palms could meet. He might have been able to pick up something if there was anything in the tower to pick up. But that was all.

He gave up. "Who did this?" he asked.

Vincent shook his head. "I don't know. I never saw them."

"Me neither," Jill added. "I was following Vincent like you said. But just before the prize-giving started, I decided to take a quick look in here. Someone must have been waiting. I didn't see anything."

"Neither did I," David muttered gloomily.

"Why *were* you following me?" Vincent asked.

Jill jerked her head in David's direction. She was unable to keep a sour tone out of her voice. "He thought you were going to steal the Grail."

Vincent nodded briefly. "That figures," he muttered.

"I knew *someone* was going to steal the Grail," David

said. He was blushing again. He had been wrong from the start, horribly wrong, and his mistake could end up killing all of them. He thought back now, remembering everything that had happened. And the words poured out. "I was set up that night in the heads' study. I wasn't trying to steal the exam. And I did know what *thanatomania* means. Somebody stole part of my answer. And what about the waxworks? Okay—maybe it wasn't you who sent them after me, but I wasn't making it up. Somebody stole the statuette so that you could win." David realized he wasn't making much sense. He slumped back into silence.

"Is that why you were against me from the start?" Vincent asked.

"I wasn't . . ."

"You never gave me a chance."

David knew it was true. He wasn't blushing because he had been wrong but because he had been cruel and stupid. He had thought the worst of Vincent for the simple reason that he didn't like him, and he didn't like him because the two of them had been in competition. Vincent was right. David had never given him a chance. They had been enemies from the start.

"How was I to know?" David muttered. "I didn't know you—"

"You never asked," Vincent said. There was a pause and he went on. "I didn't want to come here," he said. "I didn't have any parents. My dad left when I was a kid and my mother didn't want to know. They put me in an institution . . . St. Elizabeth's in Sourbridge. It was horrible. Then I got moved here." He took a deep breath. "I thought I'd be happy at Groosham Grange, especially when I found out what was really going on. All I wanted was to be one of you, to be accepted. I didn't even care about the Unholy Grail."

"I'm sorry . . ." David had never felt more ashamed.

"I did try to be friends with you, but everything I did just made it worse." He sighed. "Why did you think it was me? Why me?"

"I don't know." David thought back. "I saw you coming out of the tower," he said, knowing how lame it sounded. "And that night, when I was caught looking at the exam papers . . . did you come here then?"

Vincent nodded. "Yes."

"Why?"

Vincent thought for a moment, then answered. "I

smoke," he said. "I started smoking cigarettes when I was at Sourbridge and I've never given up."

"Smoking!" David remembered the smell. He had come across it twice, but he hadn't recognized it: stale tobacco smoke. "I don't believe it!" he said. "Smoking is crazy. It kills you. How can you be so stupid?"

"You've been pretty stupid too," Jill muttered.

David fell silent. "Yes," he agreed.

Vincent struggled with his ropes. "I suppose it's a little late now to think about giving up."

The words were no sooner spoken than there was a distant rumble, soft and low at first but building up to a sudden crash. David looked out of the window. The sky was gray, but it wasn't the color of nightfall. It was an ugly, electric gray, somehow unnatural. There was a storm closing in on Skrull Island, and sitting high up in the tower, right in the middle of it, he felt very uncomfortable indeed.

"I think—" he began.

He got no further. The whole tower suddenly trembled as if hit by a shock wave and at the same moment Jill cried out. A great chunk of wall right next to her simply fell away, leaving a gap above her head. Outside, the air swirled around in a dark vortex and rushed into the room. There was a second crash of thunder. The chamber shook again and a crack appeared in the floor between David and Vincent, the heavy flagstones ripping apart as if they were made of paper.

"What's happening?" Jill cried.

"The Grail's left the island," David shouted. "It's the end . . ."

"What are we going to do?" Vincent said.

David glanced at the door, at the symbol painted in white on the woodwork. Even if he could have reached the eye of Horus, he would have been unable to rub it out. But while it was there, there was no chance of any magic. If they were going to escape, they would have to use their own resources. He searched the floor, trying not to look at the crack. There were no broken bottles, no rusty nails, nothing that would cut through the rope. Opposite him, Vincent was struggling feverishly. He had worked his hands loose, but his wrists were still securely tied.

A third crash of thunder. This time it was the roof that was hit. As Jill screamed and rolled onto her side to protect herself, two wooden rafters crashed down, followed by what felt like a ton of dust and rubble. Vincent completely disappeared from sight and for a moment David thought he had been crushed. But then Vincent coughed and staggered onto his knees, still fighting with his ropes.

"The whole place is falling apart!" Jill shouted. "How high up are we?"

"Too high up," David shouted back. The crack in the floor had widened again. Quite soon the entire thing would give way and all three of them would fall into a tunnel of broken stone and brickwork with certain death six hundred feet below.

Then he had a thought. "Vincent!" he called out. "After the prize-giving you came in here to have a cigarette."

"Yes," Vincent admitted. "But don't tell me it's bad for my health. Not now!"

"You've got cigarettes on you?"

"David, this is no time to take it up," Jill wailed.

"Yes," Vincent said.

"What were you going to light them with?"

Vincent understood at once. For the first time, David found himself admiring the other boy and knew that if only they'd been working together from the start, none of this would have happened. Contorting his body, Vincent spilled the contents of his pockets onto the floor—a handful of coins, a pen, a cigarette lighter.

Moving with his hands tied behind his back wasn't easy. First he had to turn himself around, then grope behind him to pick up the lighter. At the same time, David shuffled across the floor, pushing himself with his feet. He stopped at the crack, feeling the floor move. Jill cried out a warning. David threw himself forward. The thunder reverberated all around—closer this time—and a whole section of the floor, the section where David had just been sitting, fell away leaving a jagged black hole. David crashed down, almost dislocating his shoulder. Far below, he heard the flagstones shatter at the bottom of the tower and breathed a sigh of relief that he hadn't fallen with them.

"Hurry!" Vincent urged him.

Bruised and aching, David maneuvered himself so that he was back to back with the other boy. For her part, Jill had edged closer to them. The whole chamber was breaking up. Nowhere was safe. But if one of them went, they would all go. There was some sort of comfort in that.

"This is going to hurt," Vincent said.

"Do it," David said.

Fumbling with his fingers, afraid he would drop it, Vincent flicked the lighter on. He had to work blind, sitting with his back to David, and there was no time to be careful. David felt the flame of the lighter sear the inside of his wrist and shouted out in pain.

"I'm sorry . . ." Vincent began.

"It's not your fault. Just keep going."

Vincent flicked the lighter back on, trying to direct the flame to where he thought the ropes must be. The wind was rushing into the chamber through the holes in the wall and ceiling. David could hear it racing around the tower. He winced as the lighter burned him once again, but this time he didn't cry out. He was grateful the flame hadn't blown out.

More brickwork fell. Jill had gone white and David thought she was going to faint, but then he saw that falling plaster had covered her from head to toe. Jill wasn't the fainting sort. "I can smell burning," she said. "It must be the rope."

"Unless it's me," David muttered.

He was straining his arms, trying to avoid the flame. It felt like he had been sitting there forever. But then there was a jerk and his hands parted. Another few seconds and he was standing up, free, the two ends of the singed rope hanging from his wrists. Next, he released Vincent. The cigarette lighter had badly burned the other boy's thumb and the side of his hand. David could see the red marks. But Vincent hadn't complained.

Then it was Jill's turn. With Vincent's help, the ropes came away quickly and then the three of them were racing across the floor even as it fell away beneath them. Soon there would be nothing left of the tower. It was as if there were some invisible creature inside the storm, devouring the stone and mortar.

David reached the door first. It was unlocked. Whoever had tied them up had been confident about their knots. Clinging to Jill, with Vincent right behind him, David made his way down the spiral staircase. About halfway down, two more flagstones fell past, narrowly missing them before shattering with an explosive crash. But the lower parts of the tower were holding up. The farther they went, the safer they became. They reached the bottom unharmed.

But when they emerged into the open air, everything had changed.

Skrull Island was black, lashed by a stinging acid rain. The clouds writhed and boiled like something in a witch's cauldron. The wind stabbed at them, hurling torn plants and grass into their faces. There was nobody in sight. To one side, the cemetery looked wild and derelict with several of its gravestones on their sides. Groosham Grange itself looked dark and dismal, like some abandoned factory. A latticework of cracks had spread across it. Many of its windows had been smashed. The ivy had been torn away and hung down, a tangled mess. There was a flash of lightning and one of the gargoyles separated from the wall, launching itself into the blackness of the sky with an explosion of broken plaster.

"The Grail . . ." Vincent began.

"It's begun its journey south," David shouted. "If it reaches Canterbury, that'll be it . . . !"

"But who took it?" Jill demanded. "If it wasn't Vincent, who was it?"

"And what can we do?" Vincent held up a hand to protect his eyes from the hurtling wind. "We've got to get it back . . . !"

"I don't know!" David cried.

But suddenly he did know. Suddenly a whole lot of things had fallen into place. He knew who had the Grail. He knew how it had been smuggled off the island. The only thing he didn't know was how he could possibly reach it.

Then Vincent grabbed his arm. "I've got an idea," he yelled.

"What?"

"We can get off the island. One of us . . ."

"Show me!" David said.

The thunder crashed again. The three of them turned and ran into the school.

It was getting very hot inside the Rolls-Royce.

Mr. Eliot ran a finger around his collar and flicked on the onboard computer showing the engine temperature. The engine's heat was normal but he was sweating. His wife was sweating. Even the leather upholstery was sweating. In the backseat, all Aunt Mildred's makeup had run and she now looked like a Sioux Indian in a rainstorm. It was very odd. The sun was shining but it was already late in the day. How could it be so warm?

"I think I'm going to faint," Mrs. Eliot muttered, and promptly did, her head crashing into the dashboard.

"Oh no!" Mr. Eliot wailed.

"Is she hurt?" Mildred asked, clutching her handbag tightly to her chest and peering over the seat.

"I don't know," Mr. Eliot replied. "But she's cracked the walnut paneling. Do you know how much that walnut paneling cost me? It took me a month's salary just to pay for the walnut paneling. And another month's salary to have it fitted!"

"I think she's dead," Mildred whispered.

Mr. Eliot poked his wife affectionately in the ear. "No. She's still breathing," he said.

By now all the windows in the Rolls-Royce had steamed up, which, as they were still driving at ninety miles per hour down the highway, made things rather difficult. But Mr. Eliot still clung grimly to the steering wheel, passing on the inside and swerving on the outside. At least he was driving on the correct side of the road.

"Why don't you turn on the air-conditioning?" Aunt Mildred suggested.

"Good thinking!" Mr. Eliot snarled. "Pure mountain air. That's what you get in a Rolls-Royce. In fact I could have bought a mountain for the amount it cost me."

"Just do it, dear," Mildred panted as her lipstick trickled over her chin.

Mr. Eliot pressed a button. There was a roar, and before either of them could react, they were engulfed in a snowstorm that rushed at them through the air-conditioning vents, filling the interior of the car. In seconds their sweat had frozen. Long icicles hung off Mr. Eliot's nose and chin. His mustache had frozen solid. The intense cold had the effect of waking Mrs. Eliot up, but by now her face had stuck to the surface of the dashboard. In the backseat, Aunt Mildred had virtually disappeared beneath a huge snowdrift that rose over her like a white blanket. The Rolls-Royce swerved left and right, sending a Fiat and a Lexus hurtling into the median. Mr. Eliot's hands were now firmly glued to the steering wheel.

"What's going on?" he screamed, his breath coming out in white clouds. "I had the car serviced before I left. It was a Rolls-Royce serviceman. And all Rolls-Royce servicemen are regularly serviced themselves. What's happening? This is motorway madness!"

"There's a service station," Aunt Mildred whimpered. "Why don't we stop for a few minutes?"

"Good idea!" Mr. Eliot agreed, and wrenched the car over to the left.

It took them ten minutes to extract themselves from

the frozen Rolls-Royce, which they left to melt slowly in the sun. Eileen Eliot had to be chiseled off the dashboard and they had to use a blowtorch to separate Edward Eliot from the steering wheel, but eventually the three of them were able to make their way up the concrete ramp that led to the Snappy Eater Café.

The Snappy Eater was a typical English highway restaurant. The tables were plastic. The chairs were plastic. And the food tasted of plastic. A few motorists were sitting in the brightly colored room, surrounded by artificial flowers, listening to the piped-in music and miserably nibbling their lukewarm snacks. Outside, the traffic roared past and the smell of burning tires and gas hung heavy in the air.

Mildred looked around and sniffed. "They have wonderful service stations in Japan," she muttered. "You can get marvelous sushi . . ."

"What's sushi?" Eileen asked. She was feeling quite carsick.

"It's raw fish!" Mildred explained enthusiastically. "Lovely strips of raw fish, all wet and jellylike. All the Japanese highway restaurants have them."

"Oh God!" Mrs. Eliot gurgled, and ran off in the direction of the toilet.

"I love Japanese food," Mildred continued, sitting down at a table and heaving her handbag in front of her.

"Why don't you shut up about Japan, you interfering old goat?" Mr. Eliot asked as he wheeled himself next to her. He snatched the menu. "Here. They've got batter-fried fish and chips. You can have that raw. Better still, you can have it battered. I'll batter you myself . . ."

A few minutes later, Eileen Eliot returned and they ordered two plates of vegetarian spaghetti and one portion of fish. But things had already begun to change inside the Snappy Eater.

Nobody noticed anything at first. The roar of the traffic drowned out the screams of the children who had been playing outside on a slide shaped like a plastic dragon. But the dragon was no longer plastic. It had already swallowed two of the children and was chasing a third with very real claws and fiery breath. About a hundred feet away, at the garage, motorists dived for cover as several of the pumps began to fire high-velocity bullets in all directions. Instead of serving unleaded octane, it seemed the pumps had decided to give out unoctaned lead.

Inside the restaurant, the piped-in music was still oozing out of the speakers—but now it really *was* oozing out. It was dripping down like honey, only bright pink and much stickier. The plastic flowers were being attacked by plastic wasps. All the waiters and waitresses had broken out in pimples. The one who was serving the Eliots had lost all his hair as well.

"Oh, goodness!" Mildred exclaimed as her meal was set in front of her. "This fish is swimming in grease!"

And it was. It appeared that the chef had neglected to kill it and the silvery cod was happily swimming in a large bowl of cold grease.

"I'm not sure about this spaghetti . . ." Eileen Eliot began. But the spaghetti was also not sure about her. It had come alive. Like an army of long white worms, it slithered and jumped out of the bowl and, giggling to itself, raced across the tabletop.

The same thing had happened to Mr. Eliot's. "Get back on my plate!" he demanded, jabbing at the table with a fork. But the spaghetti ignored him, hurrying away to join two naked and headless chickens that had just escaped from the kitchen, running out on their drumsticks.

"This place is a madhouse!" Mr. Eliot said. "Let's get out of here!"

Eileen and Mildred agreed, but even leaving the restaurant wasn't easy. The revolving doors were revolving so fast that walking into them was like walking into a food processor, and two policemen and a truck driver had already been shredded. But eventually they found an open window and climbed down into the parking lot where their car was waiting.

"This would never happen in Japan," Mildred exclaimed.

"I'll put her in the trunk!" Mr. Eliot muttered as he started the engine. "I wish I'd never brought her . . ."

"What is going on?" Eileen Eliot moaned.

The Rolls-Royce reversed over somebody's picnic and into a wastepaper basket. "Margate, here we come!" Mr. Eliot cried.

Mildred Eliot sat miserably in the backseat with her handbag beside her. Although she hadn't noticed it and probably wouldn't have mentioned it if she had, the handbag had begun to glow with a strange green light. And there was something inside it, humming softly and vibrating.

The Rolls-Royce swerved back onto the highway and continued its journey south.

David clung on for dear life, suspended between the ocean bubbling below and the storm clouds swirling above. Every gust of wind threatened to knock him off his perch and the wind never stopped. There wasn't a muscle in his body that wasn't aching and yet he couldn't relax, not for an instant. He had to concentrate. With his hands clamped in front of him, his arms rigid, his face lashed by the rain, he urged the broomstick on.

It had been Vincent's idea.

Mrs. Windergast's broomstick was the only way off the island. Even if they had been able to take Captain Bloodbath's boat, the sea was far too rough for sailing. Mrs. Windergast had taught them the basic theory of broomstick flying. True, they had never tried it before and certainly not in a full-blown storm. But as soon as Vincent had suggested it, David knew it was the only way.

They had taken the broomstick from Mrs. Windergast's room. Normally the door would have been locked and the room would certainly have been protected by a magic spell. But everything had changed in the storm. The staff and pupils had vanished, taking shelter in the caverns below while the elements—the sea, the wind, the lightning and the rain—joined forces to destroy the island. Mrs. Windergast's room was empty, but one of the windows had been shattered and pools of water and broken glass covered the carpet. There were papers everywhere. The curtains flapped madly against the wall. The broomstick lay on its side, half hidden by a chair.

"You know where you're going?" Jill called out. She had to raise her voice to make herself heard above the storm.

David nodded. A half-remembered line here and a few spoken words there had come together and everything had clicked. He had worked it out.

His parents. After they left Groosham Grange, they were taking Mildred back to her home in Margate. Edward Eliot had told him as much in the letter he had written a few weeks before. And where was Margate? Just a few miles north of Canterbury.

And what had Aunt Mildred said as she got into the car? *I'm sure it wasn't as heavy as this when I set out . . .* She had lost her handbag. It had been handed back to her—but heavier than before. David was certain. Somebody had hidden the Grail inside the handbag. And she had unwittingly carried it off the island.

Clutching the broomstick in Mrs. Windergast's room, David knew that he had to fly south, somehow find the orange Rolls-Royce and intercept it before it reached Margate. Someone would be waiting for it at the other end. But who? That was still a mystery.

"Be careful," Vincent said. "It's not as easy as it looks."

"And hurry, David," Jill added. "The school's powers are failing. If the Grail gets too close to Canterbury, the broomstick won't fly. You'll fall. You'll be killed."

Feeling slightly ridiculous, David pushed the broomstick between his legs with the twigs poking out behind. How had Mrs. Windergast done it? He concentrated and almost at once felt the stick pushing upward. His feet left the floor and then he wasn't exactly flying but wobbling above the carpet, trying to keep his balance.

"Good luck," Vincent said.

David turned around in midair. "Thanks," he said. Then he and the broomstick lurched out of the window and into the storm.

The first few minutes were the worst. The wind seemed to be coming at him from all directions, invisible fists that punched at him again and again. The rain blinded him. He knew he was climbing higher but in what direction, north or south, he couldn't say. The broomstick worked through some sort of telepathy. He only had to think "right" to go that way. But if he thought too hard, the broomstick would spin around like an amusement-park ride and it was as much as he could do to hang on. He glimpsed Groosham Grange, rising at a crazy angle from the corner of his eye. Then it was upside down! He had to get his bearings. He felt sick and exhausted and the journey hadn't even begun. He forced the broomstick up the right way. With his body tensed, he resisted the force of the storm. He was about three hundred feet up. And at last he had control.

And so he flew. The broomstick had no speed limit and seemed to have left the island behind in only seconds. The Norfolk coastline was already visible ahead. He relaxed, then yelled out as he collided with a flock of seagulls. Again he was blinded, aware only of gray feathers and indignant cries all around him. The control was broken and the broomstick plunged down, pulling David after it, his stomach lurching. The sea rushed up to swallow him.

"Up!" David shouted, and thought it too, clamping his mind on it. Despite everything, he didn't panic. Already he understood that panic would freeze his mind and without a clear mind he couldn't fly. He relaxed everything, even his hands. And at once the broomstick responded. It had swooped down but now it curved gently up. The sea had gone. As the broomstick rose higher, David saw dry land below, the sandy beaches of the Norfolk coast. He had left the storm behind him. The sun was shining.

Swallowing hard, he turned the broomstick south and set off in pursuit of the Unholy Grail.

After David had gone, Vincent and Jill left Mrs. Windergast's room and made their way downstairs, heading for the network of underground caves beneath the school. The wind was still howling outside and as they reached the main staircase a huge stained-glass window suddenly exploded inward, showering them with multi-colored fragments of glass. They ran into the library, intending to pass through the mirror that concealed the passage down—but the windows in the room had been shattered by the storm and the mirror had broken too. A single crack ran down its face, effectively sealing it. Jill knew that if they tried to pass through a cracked mirror, they would be cut in half.

"Outside!" Vincent shouted. Jill nodded and followed him.

It was even worse outside than they had imagined.

The entire island was in the grip of something like a volcanic eruption. Whole trees had been torn up, the gravestones in the cemetery blown apart, the larger tombs thrown open. The sky was midnight black, crossed and recrossed by streaks of lightning that were like razor blades slashing at the air. The whole of the East Tower had collapsed in on itself. The rest of the school looked as if it was about to do the same.

"Look!" Jill pointed and Vincent followed her finger to the gargoyles that surrounded Groosham Grange. Their eyes were shining, bright red in the darkness, like warning lights before a nuclear explosion. At the same time, something huge and terrifying was rising up in the far distance behind the school. Jill had only just seen what it was before Vincent had grabbed her, throwing her into the safety of one of the tombs.

It was a tidal wave. The whole world disappeared in a silver-gray nightmare as the wave pounded down on the school, completely engulfing the cemetery, the woods, everything. A second later, the ground was shaken by some awful convulsion below and Jill found herself thrown into Vincent's arms.

"How much longer?" she cried. "How much more can the school take?"

Vincent had gone quite pale. He was cold and soaking wet, drenched by the water that had found its way into the tomb. "I don't know," he said. "The Grail must be getting closer to Canterbury." He looked up into the pitch-black sky. "Come on, David," he whispered. "We're running out of time."

The power of the Unholy Grail was growing steadily. And it was becoming more unpredictable and more out of control the farther it was taken from Groosham Grange.

"I feel very peculiar," Mildred was saying. "It must be something I ate. I'm blowing up all over."

Eileen Eliot turned around and looked into the back of the car. The small, shriveled woman was expanding as if someone had connected her to an air hose. Her handbag lay next to her, humming and glowing brilliantly. Mildred's shoulders and chest had torn through her clothes and she had lost a great deal of her hair. There was also something rather odd about her eyes. "It's true, Edward," Eileen squeaked. "I think we'd better take her to a doctor."

But Edward Eliot ignored her. He himself had changed

during the last few minutes. His skin had become thicker, pinker. His hands and face were covered unevenly with bristles and his ears and nose had changed shape.

"Edward . . . ?" Eileen quavered.

Mr. Eliot snorted and stamped his foot down on the accelerator. Except he no longer had a foot. His shoe had come off to reveal what looked remarkably like a pig's trotter.

Eileen Eliot slumped in her seat and began to cry. All around her, the entire world was bending and twisting out of shape as the familiar turned into the insane.

One moment they were approaching a zebra crossing. Then the air seemed to shimmer and a moment later a whole herd of zebras had emerged in a stampede from a post office. Cat's eyes set in the tarmac disappeared as the cats—panthers, jaguars and tigers—leaped out to terrorize the unfortunate people of Margate. Traffic lights sprouted wings and flew off. A humpback bridge spouted a great spray of water before being harpooned by a party of Icelandic tourists.

Inside the handbag, the Unholy Grail hummed and glimmered.

Mildred's dress tore in half. She was enormous now,

and when she spoke again, it was not English that came out of her lips. It was Japanese. Her cheeks bulged and her great, fat legs stuck out like tree stumps.

Eileen Eliot realized what had happened. Aunt Mildred had always loved the Japanese. Now she had become one. A sumo wrestler.

"Edward . . ." she wept.

Mr. Eliot snorted again. He was no longer able to speak. His mouth and nose had molded themselves together and jutted forward over what was left of his chin. His teeth had also doubled in size. The sleeves of his jacket and shirt had torn open to reveal two pink knotted arms, covered in the same spiky hair that bristled out of his neck and face.

Edward Eliot had always been a road hog. And so the Unholy Grail had turned him into one.

Eileen Eliot took one look at him and screamed. "This can't be happening!" she whimpered. "It's horrible. Horrible! I wish I was ten thousand miles from here."

The Unholy Grail heard her. There was a sudden *whoosh!* and she felt herself being sucked out of the car in a tunnel of green light, her clothes being torn off as she went. For a few seconds the whole world disappeared. Then she was falling, screaming all the way. The ground rushed up at her and the next thing she knew she was standing in a pool of cold and muddy water that reached up to her waist.

Mrs. Eliot had traveled thousands of miles. She was standing in a nice paddy in China, surrounded by some very surprised Chinese rice farmers. Mrs. Eliot smiled and fainted.

Mr. Eliot had seen his wife disappear. He turned and stared at the empty seat . . . not a good idea at seventy miles an hour. The next thing he knew, the car had left the road and crashed into a lamppost. Of course, he hadn't bothered with a seat belt and he was hurled, snorting and squealing, through the very expensive smoked-glass front window, out onto the pavement. Wedged in the back, her huge stomach trapped by the front seat, Aunt Mildred was unable to move. But at least her flesh had cushioned her from the impact.

The back door of the Rolls-Royce had been torn open in the collision and Mildred's handbag had rolled out. It lay on the pavement, glowing more powerfully than ever. Awkwardly, Mildred poked an arm out and tried to reach it. But before her podgy fingers could close on the bag, someone appeared, leaning down to snatch it away.

Mildred gazed at the figure in astonishment. "You!" she said.

But then the person had gone. And the handbag had gone too.

Far below him, David could see the chaos that was the center of Margate and knew with a surge of excitement that he was getting closer. He was flying at six hundred feet—high enough, he hoped, not to be seen from the ground but low enough to avoid any passing planes. He had had one nasty fright as he had crossed the Thames Estuary at Sheerness and a DC-10 taking off from City Airport had cut right in front of him. There had also been some unpleasant air currents to negotiate over the flat Suffolk countryside. But he was almost there. He had done it.

But the worst surprise was still to come.

David had flown inland, leaving Margate behind him. He was actually beginning to enjoy the journey, the rush of the wind in his hair, the complete silence, the sense of freedom as he soared through the late-afternoon sunlight. The broomstick was responding instantly to the slightest suggestion. Up, down, left, right—he only had to think it and he was away.

Then suddenly it stopped.

David's stomach lurched as the broomstick plummeted down and it was only by forcing his thoughts through his clenched hands and into the wooden shaft that he was able to regain control. The broomstick continued forward but more hesitantly. Then it shuddered and dipped again. David knew his worst fear had been realized. Just as Jill had warned, the Grail was approaching Canterbury. And the closer it got, the less powerful he became. Groosham Grange with all its magic was falling apart—and that included the broomstick. It was like a car running out of gas. He could actually feel it coughing and stammering beneath him. How much farther could he go?

And then he saw the cathedral. It stood at the far end of a sprawling modern town, separated from it by a cluster of houses and a swath of perfectly mown grass. The cathedral stretched from east to west, a glinting pile of soaring towers, arched windows and silver-white roofs that looked, from this height, like some absurdly expensive miniaturized model. It was there, only a few miles away. David urged the broomstick on. It surged obediently forward but then dropped another hundred feet. David could feel its power running out.

The broomstick reached the main street of Canterbury and followed it up and over the elegant Christ Church Gate and past the cathedral itself. David found himself high above the central tower. Looking down, he could see right into the cloisters. He could hear organ music drifting through the stone walls. Leaning to one side, he tilted around, looking for somewhere to land.

And that was when the broom's power failed. There was nothing he could do. Like a wounded bird he fell out of the sky, spinning around and around, still clinging to the useless broomstick that was now above his head. The cathedral had disappeared, whipped out of his field of vision. He could see the grass rushing up at him, a solid green wall.

David turned once in the air, cried out, then hit the ground and lay still.

He was still alive. He knew because of the pain. David wasn't sure how many bones there were in the human body, but it felt as if he had broken every one of them. He was surprised he could even move.

He was lying on the grass like one of those chalk drawings the police make after a murder. His arms and legs were sticking out at strange angles. His head was pounding and he could taste blood where he had bitten his tongue. But he was still breathing. He guessed that at the last minute the broomstick must have slowed his fall. Otherwise he wouldn't have been on the grass—he would have been underneath it.

He opened his eyes and looked around him. He had

landed in the very middle of the cathedral close. On one side of him there was a wooden building—the Cathedral Welcome Center—and a couple of trees. Behind there was a row of houses that included the Cathedral Shop. The cathedral itself was in front of him, above him, looming over him.

It began with two towers that at some time had become home to a family of black ragged birds. Ravens or crows perhaps. They were swooping in and out of the pointed windows, launching themselves into the sky. Then there were two lines of smaller towers, so intricately carved that they looked like something that might have grown at the bottom of the sea. At the far end there was a taller tower. It stood poised like a medieval rocket about to be launched. The sun was trapped behind it, low in the sky.

The sun . . .

With an effort, David sat up and saw that this third tower was casting a shadow that stretched out across the lawn, stopping only a few yards from where he lay. At the same time he saw somebody moving toward him.

The solitary figure walked steadily forward. David squinted, raising himself on his arm. The pain made him cry out, but he still couldn't see who it was. He was blinded by the light shafting into his eyes and he was still dizzy and disorientated after his fall.

"Hello, David," Mr. Helliwell said.

Mr. Helliwell.

He should have known all along.

David had suspected Vincent because Vincent was new. But so was Mr. Helliwell. He had joined the staff at Groosham Grange at about the same time. Again, he had believed it was Vincent who had stolen one of his exam papers because Vincent had collected them. But who had he handed them to? Mr. Helliwell. With his voodoo powers, it would have been easy for the teacher to animate the waxworks and, of course, he had been part of the contest in London from the start. Always Mr. Helliwell. He had befriended David's parents at the prize-giving and it had been he who had found Aunt Mildred's lost handbag.

"Are you surprised to see me?" Mr. Helliwell asked, and smiled. In his ragged black suit, top hat and tails, he looked like some sort of crazy scarecrow or perhaps a circus entertainer down on his luck.

"No," David said.

"I never thought you'd escape from the East Tower," the voodoo teacher said. He glanced at the fallen broomstick. "I presume that's Mrs. Windergast's," he went on. "You really have been very resourceful, David. Very brave. I'm sorry it's all been for nothing."

He brought his hand up and now David saw the Unholy Grail nestling in his huge palm. David tried to move but there was nothing he could do. It was just the two of them and the Unholy Grail. The cathedral had shut down for the evening and the close itself was empty. The sun was creeping down toward the horizon and the whole building was shining with a soft golden light. But the shadows were still sharp. The shadow from the third, single spire was as clear as ever, edging closer toward him as the sun set. All Mr. Helliwell had to do was hold out his arm. The Unholy Grail would pass into the shadow of Canterbury Cathedral. Groosham Grange would fall.

"It's the end, David," Mr. Helliwell said, his voice low and almost sad. "In a way, I'm glad you're here to see it. Of course, once I pass the Grail into the shadow, you'll crumble into dust. But I always liked you. I want you to know that."

"Thanks," David muttered through gritted teeth.

"Well. I suppose we'd better get it over with." The

hand holding the Grail moved slowly. The Grail passed through the last of the sunlight.

"Wait!" David shouted. "There's one thing I want to know!"

Mr. Helliwell hesitated. The Grail glittered in his hand only inches from the shadow of the cathedral.

"You've got to tell me," David said. He tried to stand but his legs were still too weak. "Why did you do it?"

Mr. Helliwell considered. He looked up at the sky. "There's still thirty minutes' sunlight," he said. "If you think you can trick me, boy . . ."

"No, no." David shook his head. Even that hurt him. "You're far too clever for me, Mr. Helliwell. I admit it. But I've got a right to know. Why did you set me up? Why did Vincent have to win the Unholy Grail?"

"All right." Mr. Helliwell relaxed, lowering the Grail. But the shadow stayed there, hungry, inching ever closer.

"When I started making my plans, I didn't care who won the Unholy Grail," Mr. Helliwell began. "But then I happened to see that letter from your father." David remembered. He had dropped it in the corridor, after the fight with Vincent. Mr. Helliwell had picked it up.

"When I saw that your parents were coming to the prize-giving and then going on to Margate, it was too good an opportunity to miss. Somehow I'd slip it into their luggage and they'd carry it off for me. Nobody would suspect.

"But then I realized that I couldn't let you win it, David. If you had the Grail and then it disappeared, your parents would have been stopped before they got anywhere near the jetty. People would assume you'd given it to them. But Vincent was perfect. He had no parents, no relatives. While everyone was looking for him, nobody would be looking for you or for anyone connected with you."

"So you sent the waxworks."

"Yes. I followed you to London. I was always there."

"But there's still one thing you haven't told me." The pain in David's shoulder and leg was getting worse. He wondered if he could stop himself from passing out. At the same time, his mind was racing. Was he completely helpless? Did he have any power left? "Why did you do it, Mr. Helliwell?" he asked. "Why?"

The teacher laughed, a booming, hollow laugh tinged with malice. "I know what you're thinking," he said.

"You really believe you can catch me off guard?" Mr. Helliwell reached out with his foot and pushed David back down on to the grass. David cried out and the world swam in front of his eyes, but still he forced himself to stay conscious. "You are searching for magic, boy. But you have none. We've talked enough. It's time for you to join the dust of the earth . . ."

The Grail came up again.

"Why did you do it?" David shouted. "You were the best. One of the great voodoo magicians. You couldn't have faked that. You were famous . . ."

"I was converted!" Mr. Helliwell snapped out the three words, and even as he spoke them a strange light came into his eyes. "An English missionary—the Bishop of Bletchley—came to Haiti and I met him. My first thought was to turn him into a toad or a snake or a watermelon. But then we got talking. We talked for hours. And he showed me the error of my ways."

"What do you mean?"

"All my life I had been evil, child. Like you. Like everyone at Groosham Grange. He persuaded me that it was time to do good. To crush the school and to kill everybody in it."

"That doesn't sound very good to me," David remarked. "Crushing and killing! What had we ever done to you?"

"You were evil!"

"That's nonsense!" And even as David began to speak he at last understood what Mr. Fitch and Mr. Teagle had been trying to tell him. The difference between good and evil.

"Groosham Grange isn't evil," he went on. "It's just different—that's all. Monsieur Leloup may be a werewolf and Mr. Kilgraw may be a vampire, but that's not their fault. They were born that way. And what about Mr. Creer? Just because he's a ghost, it doesn't mean he hasn't got a right to be left in peace!"

"Evil!" Mr. Helliwell insisted.

"Look who's talking!" David replied. "You're the one who's been lying and cheating. You're the one who pushed me out of the tower—and when that didn't work, you tied me up and left me to die. You stole the Unholy Grail—my parents have probably been disintegrated by now—and you've also destroyed half of Margate. You may think you're some sort of saint, Mr. Helliwell, but the truth is you probably did less damage when you were a full-fledged black magician back on Haiti!"

"You don't know what you're saying, boy . . ." Mr. Helliwell's face had grown pale and there was a dull red flicker in his eyes. "I did what I did for the good of mankind."

"It doesn't matter why you did it or who you did it for," David insisted. "It's easy enough to say that, isn't it? But when you stop and think about what you're doing . . . that's different. You're crushing and killing. You said it yourself. And I don't think that makes you a saint, Mr. Helliwell. I think it makes you a monster and a fanatic."

"I . . . I . . . I . . ." Mr. Helliwell was beside himself with rage. His eyes were bulging and one corner of his mouth twitched. He tried to speak, but only saliva flecked over his lips. "Enough!" he hissed. "I've listened to enough!"

Mr. Helliwell raised the Unholy Grail. For a moment it caught the sun, magnifying it and splintering it into a dazzling ball of red light. The shadow cast by the one, solitary spire reached out for the Grail.

And David pushed.

In the last few seconds he had formed a plan and had stored up all his remaining strength to make it work. He had argued with the teacher to keep him busy, to divert his attention from what was about to happen. *Because as long as the Unholy Grail was out of the shadow, some power remained.* David used that power now. Guided by him, Mrs. Windergast's broomstick suddenly leaped off the grass and hurtled, faster than a bullet, toward Mr. Helliwell's head.

The teacher ducked. The broomstick whipped over his shoulder and continued its journey up.

"Missed!" Mr. Helliwell threw back his head and laughed. "So that was what you were trying? Well, it didn't work, David. And so . . . good-bye!"

With a malevolent smile, he jerked his arm out, thrusting the Unholy Grail into the shadow of Canterbury Cathedral.

But the shadow was no longer there.

Mr. Helliwell frowned and looked down at the grass. The sun was shining, uninterrupted by the spire.

"What . . . ?" he began.

He looked up.

When David had sent the broomstick on its final journey, he hadn't been aiming at the voodoo teacher. Its flight had continued, over the man's head and up into the air, toward the cathedral. It had found its target in the church spire, and strengthened by David's magic, the wooden handle had passed clean through the stone, slicing it in half. The top of the spire had been cut off. The sun had been allowed through. The Unholy Grail was still protected by its light.

"You—" Mr. Helliwell growled.

He never finished the sentence. The broomstick had sliced through a ton of stone. The top of the spire, a massive chunk that tapered to a point, crashed down.

It landed on Mr. Helliwell.

David couldn't look. He heard a single, high-pitched scream, then a sickening thud. Something fell onto the grass, next to his hand. He reached out and took it. It was the Unholy Grail.

Moving slowly, David forced himself up on to his feet and staggered away from the rubble, taking the Grail with him. Every movement hurt him. After every step he had to stop and catch his breath. But soon he was away from the shadow of Canterbury Cathedral, and pressing the Grail against his chest, he continued on through the safety of the dying evening light.

The waves rolled in toward Skrull Island, glittering in the morning sun, then broke—silver—on the slanting rocks. A gentle breeze wafted over the shoreline, tracing patterns in the sand. Everything was peaceful. Butterflies danced in the warm sunshine and the air was filled with the scent of flowers.

It was actually the first week of December and the rest of England was covered by snow, with biting winds and cloudy skies. But the magic had returned to Groosham Grange along with the Unholy Grail. And after all the excitement, Mr. Fitch and Mr. Teagle had decided to give everyone three weeks' extra summer sun as a reward.

The school had been quickly restored. The moment the Grail had been put back in its right place, Groosham Grange had risen out of the rubble as proud and as strong as it had been before. Indeed, there were even a few improvements. Several of the classrooms had repainted themselves in the process and a new computer wing had mysteriously risen out of the swampland that lay to the west of the cemetery.

The staff had also been busy. It had taken a long and complicated spell to repair all the damage that had been done to both Margate and to Canterbury Cathedral, but they had managed it. Then they had made everyone involved—from the waiters and waitresses at the Snappy Eater to the police and ordinary citizens—forget everything that had happened. The Eliots and Aunt Mildred had been restored and returned home. It was small wonder that the entire school was in need of a vacation.

Two months had passed since David's flight to Canterbury. He was sitting now in Mr. Kilgraw's darkened study, one leg in a cast, his face still bruised and pale. The assistant headmaster was sitting opposite him. "So have you come to a decision?" he asked.

"Yes, sir," David said. "I've decided I want to leave the school."

Mr. Kilgraw nodded but said nothing. A chink of sunlight spilled through a crack in the curtain and he glanced at it distastefully. "May I ask why?" he said.

David thought for a moment. It seemed to him that he had been thinking about what he was going to say for weeks. But now that it was time to put it into words, he wasn't so sure. "I do like it here," he said. "I've been very happy. But . . ." He drew a breath. "I just think I've had enough magic. I feel I've learned everything I want to learn and now it's time to go back into the real world."

"To learn about life."

"Yes. I suppose so. And anyway . . ." This was the difficult part. "When I look back at what happened with Vincent and everything, I still think I was to blame. The truth is, I really wanted the Unholy Grail. I wanted it more than anything I've ever wanted in my life and that made me behave . . . badly." He broke off. The words sounded so feeble somehow. "I'm worried about how I behaved," he concluded. "And so I think it's time to go."

"Maybe you want to learn more about yourself," Mr. Kilgraw said.

"I suppose so."

The assistant headmaster stood up, and to David's surprise, he was smiling. "You're a very remarkable young man," he said. "Our top student. The rightful winner of the Unholy Grail. And you're right. We've taught you everything you need to know. We already knew that. Why do you think we allowed all this to happen?"

It took David a few seconds to play back what Mr. Kilgraw had just said and understand the meaning. "You knew about Mr. Helliwell!" he stammered.

"We knew more than perhaps we pretended. But, you see, we had to be sure that you were ready. Think of it as one final test. Before your departure."

"But . . ." David's mind was reeling. "The Grail! Canterbury Cathedral! He came so close . . ."

The smile on Mr. Kilgraw's face broadened. "We had complete faith in you, David. We knew you wouldn't let us down."

He went over to the door and opened it. David stood up, supporting himself on a stick. "Where do you think you'll go?" Mr. Kilgraw asked.

"Well, I'm not going home, if that's what you mean," David said. "I thought I'd see a bit of the world. Mrs. Windergast says that Tibet is very interesting at this time of the year . . ."

"You'll fly?"

"Yes." Now it was David's turn to smile. "But not on a plane."

Mr. Kilgraw held out a hand. "Good luck," he said. "And remember, we'll always be here if you need us. Make sure you keep in touch."

They shook hands. David left the study and went back outside. One of the lower classes was out on the lawn—or rather, as they were practicing levitation, just above it. Gregor, who had been trying to get a suntan, was sitting in a deck chair, his body gently smoking. The sun was still high in the sky. David followed the path over to the top of the cliffs. His favorite place on the island.

Vincent and Jill were waiting for him, sitting together, looking at the waves.

"Did you tell him?" Jill asked as he arrived.

"Yes."

"What did he say?"

"He wished me luck."

"You'll probably need it," Vincent said. "I'm sorry you're going, David. I'll really miss you."

"I'll miss you too, Vincent. And you, Jill. In fact I'll even miss Gregor. But I expect we'll meet again. Somehow I don't think I've heard the last of Groosham Grange."

Vincent nodded and stood up. Jill took David's arm. And together the three friends walked down toward the sea.